Anamnesis

Anamnesis

Stephen G. Faulkner

1

It was getting late when Jack and Sue got on the road, the summer sun sinking, lighting the sky in copper hues. They travel in a beige battered station wagon, the kids have left home, but the family car remains. They are late for their eldest's dinner party and the mood is tense.

"We would have been on the road hours ago if we didn't have to put up with this wretched car breaking down."

"New cars breakdown too you know, and I could never sell Betsy you know that, she's a member of the family."

"I already have to put up with one unreliable member of the family, this one I could happily lose."

Jack did not reply, learning not to perpetuate the argument as he knows Sue is in no mood to let him have the last word.

Through the country lanes between towns, Betsy lurches over a crest and tips into a tight left turn, "We are already late, so arriving in one piece would be nice." Silence.. They are just about to travel along a long straight piece of road when suddenly they stop, no jolting, no being thrown to the windscreen, just halted, a blue/white light fills the air and they watch the trees fall away beside the car, as it is taken at increasing speeds, tearing through wispy cloud to a saucer many miles in the sky.

Up here the sun reappears, lighting the side of this alien craft bright white. First far away now ever larger as they are zipped along this light beam, till they are now right next to it. Slowing as they finally approach, they are taken into the bowels of the ship, doors close beneath them, as the car settles against the floor of the craft, Jack is apprehensive, Sue is livid.

2

Two alien creatures, or people.. approach the car, they are wispy thin with large egg shaped heads and huge dark eyes. They look like every other description of an alien, due to the fact that that is what aliens look like. They scan around the car looking for means of entry, tentatively touching the doors and windows and hood. Jack sits stone still his eyes follow their movements. Sue says, "I'll open it then, you useless skinny buggers." and flings the door open, startling the two aliens, who jump back, "What the hell do you think your doing just pulling people up to your space ship willy nilly?!, what gives you the right to…" Sue is cut short by a jab from a long pole that when it touched her stopped her movement and sound entirely. "Sorry for that," said Preep, the slightly shorter alien to Jack "She was getting very agitated." Jack quietly gets out, not thinking of how useful that rod was at all.

Stroop and Preep talk to each other in their own language for a time, in whistles and clicks, but even to unknowing ears they did not seem very happy with their choice of abductees. Stroop turns to Jack and says, "We will be taking you back to our planet for assessment, but will return you, and most do not even remember participating in our program." He turns and glances at Sue, turning back to Jack "Will you be able to control your mate?"

"If you give me that stick maybe, but otherwise you had better think of a very good reason she is missing her eldest's birthday."

"We are merely doing what we are told, we all have our job we must do, we are being as nice about it as we can, does she like cake?"

"Well yes, but.."

"Very well, we have cake." Stroop nods to Preep and he leaves to get the cake. Worth a try Jack supposes.

Preep holds the cake while Stroop touches the device to Sue, "..take innocent people away.."

"Cake?" Preep asks as he offers it to Sue, with a wave of her hand Sue launches the cake into the air.

"No I don't want your poisonous ca.." Another touch of the rod and Sue is still again, the cake hits the floor.

Preep looks at Stroop and wanders off to get some sort of cleaning apparatus. Jack turned to Stroop "Look, I understand you are doing your job and all that, but Sue is not one to be intimidated or scared at such weirdness, can you not go back and get someone else?"

"That would be nice, but it does not work like that, we are already on our way."

Stroop touches the prod to Sue and runs for the door.

"..ke… where did they go?" Jack looked down at the cake, "You were scaring them so they ran off and left you with me."

"Why would they be scared? They are the evil little abductors, we are the victims here."

"They are just doing their job, they would take us back if they could, but they can't. We should just make the best of it."

"The best of it?! We are being kidnapped by aliens and you want to treat it like a holiday trip."

Jack, Sue and Betsy are in a large room, walls of metal of some kind unpainted and the floor the same. A dirtier place than you'd expect, even discounting the cake strewn across the floor. The door through which Stroop and Preep escaped being metal too, with a small porthole window to check the goings on on the other side of it. Sue walks over to the small window and glares through it, though there is no one there to glare at, just a small corridor of which she cannot see much at all.

"If you do manage to overpower them, then what? how many space ships have you flown?" Jack reasons.

"I'll just maim them enough to convince them flying us back is a very good idea."

"But we may miss something amazing, they said they would bring us back."

"In how many pieces Jack? You are so gullible."

"Is an alien encounter and travel to other planets really worse than a dinner party?"

Even Sue can't be angry indefinitely, so she paces, and Jack keeps out of her way, eventually she calms to a mild simmer.

The metal door opens and a pair of faces meekly look around the opening to check their little hangar is still in one piece. Preep sidles past Stroop with his cleaner and goes to clean up the cake. Stroop approaches Jack, "We have some food, if you would like to follow me."

Turning to Sue Jack says "Lets have something to eat, they wouldn't poison us, they could have done whatever to us by now.."

"Do you have anymore of that cake? But watch your step, I have my eye on you," Sue warns Stroop.

"Yes yes, cake is very popular," a brightening Stroop replied.

"What do you mean by that?"

"It's .. nice cake."

"It had better be," Sue wasps.

They follow Stroop into the corridor while Preep finishes the cleaning. As with the hangar the corridor looks well used, a working ship. Turning left they enter a small room, the lighting bright, the corners of the room emitting light in some way, though one corner flickers till Preep gives a box on the wall a thump. In the centre is a table, next to it some stools fixed to the floor, on the table are some cakes and some unidentified meat on plates. Jake looks to Stroop "Could you tell me where the toilets are please? It's been a rather stressful evening and my bladder is not as strong as it used to be."

"Oh yes, to unload your waste. Your mate too?"

"Please."

"The first few times we had guests, we presumed you just did it in your clothing. As they usually did." Stroop gestures, then leads them to the small room adjacent, where two pipes sprout from the floor with funnels on top. Stroop stands at the doorway and retrieves a note pad from a wall mounting and begins taking notes as Jack and Sue eye up the 'arrangements'. Sue spotted this and looks aghast, "Bugger off! you're not watching!"

"But this interests our superiors, to gather information on your speci…"

"OUT!"

Stroop sighs and leaves them to it, only returning to poke his head round the door when he hears some commotion and some strained sucking noises from the toilet device.

Finally they return a little flustered but relieved to the mess room, both taking a seat at the table. They survey the food then Jack asks "So what meat is this?"

Preep replies "It's all of your world, as our meat may kill or distress you, we have some chicken there, here some cow and here we have dog and horse".

Silently they take some chicken each.

"Are we nearly there yet," asks Jack.

This seems to shock Preep a little,

"Oh no, it will take several weeks to get back to Knool."

Sue is not at all impressed.. "Weeks!?! this is an alien space ship, can't you hyperspace to other worlds?"

"We go as fast as we can, the distance is great, and this is an old ship.." he trailed off.

It is a very old ship, some of Preep's friends are traveling to new worlds greater distances away in brand new ships, with much better plumbing.

"What are we going to do for weeks?" asks Jack.

"We have a games room. When you have eaten I will show you, you will enjoy it," Preep said in what he hopes is an enthusiastic tone.

The games room is small, very small, smaller than the bathroom. Two chairs with helmets attached to each one by a tangle of wires. Obviously some sort of virtual reality system. "No TV?" enquires Sue.

"I'll give it a go," says Jack and makes himself comfortable in the chair. Preep takes the huge oversized helmet and places it on Jack's head, it wobbles and knocks his neck until Preep adjusts it. He then flicks a switch and a low hum begins to emanate from the machinery, as Jack begins his journey.

Jack finds himself sat on a beach of snow white sand, the clear blue sea gently laps the shore. He can hear gulls screech and smell the ozone. So he stands and takes a walk, kicking the sand, then removes his shoes so he can feel the sand between his toes, almost under his breath he says, "You should try this Sue, it's amazing." From the ether Sue replies "I have never liked computer games, they're for the children."

"Oh but you must! This is incredible." He hears a sigh and some clattering and in a few minutes Sue appears on the beach. She appears impressed at first, but it takes more to impress a Sue, "It is realistic yes, but none of it is real, everything is just in our heads from their box of tricks."

"Well I'm going to go imagine a pub over there," and he wanders up the beach towards some parasols. Sue takes a seat on the beach and plays with the sand beneath her feet, feeling every grain roll. Then she gets up and walks in the direction that Jack walked.

3

In the flight room Stroop is sat at the console, watching the light flicker, and checking the numbers on screens are as they should be. Preep enters and sits beside him and put his feet up on the console, lacing his long slender fingers across his stomach and sighs. They speak their alien clicks and whistles, which if we understood their language, we would have heard Stroop say "Have our guests settled in the recreation room?"

"Yes Stroop, even the wild one has settled, they don't seem as perturbed as the others, but these are more saggy than our previous guests, maybe when they go saggy they are no longer surprised by unusual events."

"With age comes sag, and from sag comes calm."

"You are wise sometimes Preep."

Sue finds Jack sat at an outdoor bar with a beer, she is not impressed at the barmaid at all.. "Could you have imagined any bigger boobs?"

"I didn't imagine any of this, I don't think that is how it works" the barmaid turns to Sue, "What would you like?"

"I'll just have a lemonade, I want to keep a clear head."

"Ha ha, so it is real now?"

"Shut up..," she says, takes her drink, then takes a seat next to Jack and relaxes to take in the view.

Both Sue and Jack are in their mid sixties, Sue an ex teacher and Jack a soon to be retired engineer. Jack is a little shorter than Sue. Sue enjoys being the larger lady and the bigger personality, still wearing heels as punctuation. They have three grown children. Their eldest John, an accountant, living in a fine home with his new wife Julie. Jenny the middle daughter, a nurse living in an apartment with her girlfriend. And the youngest, Sean, an artist of sorts who finally moved out last year.

As the pair sit, the sun is being quenched in the ocean, painting the most beautiful picture in orange hues.
"When was the last time we had a holiday? Jack asks, "Not just a break, a proper holiday, away from it all?"

"Well, that would probably be when Sean wanted to go to Disneyland, so about fifteen, twenty years ago?"

"Too long."

They ordered a margarita each and continued to watch the view change with another drink, then another.

Then got a little merry, and got a little sand in places they hadn't got it in years.

Then they fell asleep on the beach.

4

Dreams of sand drift away as the conscious mind starts to awaken. First Jack's eyes open, he gazes at the dark metal wall and feels his aching body, a body stiff from sleeping in an upright chair. Looking next to him, there still asleep, drool escaping the corner of her mouth, his wife sat snoring. The helmets had been removed once they were asleep, to take the weight off their necks.

Jack leans over and gently holds her shoulder. She wakes in a snort and surveys the same grey walls, "Oh, why wasn't this the dream?" Jack had only eyes of concern in reply.

They both get up and stretched their tired stiff limbs and wander into the hall, time to explore this place and maybe learn a thing or two thought Jack. He had seen Preep opening a door, so pressed his fingers to the same pads on the control, on the second attempt the door opens, and inside they find what turns out to be this flying saucer's 'Cupboard under the stairs'. All sorts of cleaners and dusters stacked on top of each other haphazardly, nothing of great interest. Sue notes to herself that nothing looked very weapon-y to her. Jack closes the door and they quietly continue their exploration, "Just a minute," said Sue, "I recognise this one." She opens the door and says to Jack "Won't be a minute."

"I'll go after you," replied Jack.

Jack exits the toilet just as Stroop appeared around the bend in the corridor.

"Careful where you go, a little knowledge can get you into a lot of trouble."

Sue does not like his tone, "A little knowledge is very useful in the right place."

"This is not the right place, please be careful as none of us wish to be evacuated into space, certainly not at this speed. Come, follow me, I shall guide you safely."

They follow Stroop around the corridor to the flight room. He opens the door, Preep is already there, he quickly takes his feet down from the console and stands to greet the visitors. "I always like to see this part of the journey," says Stroop as he presses a button on the console and part of the metal wall slides away revealing an expansive window.

Preep dims the lights in the control room, leaving just the blinking of the lights on the console. Through the window the stars come alive, pure bright and of all colours, moving gracefully towards them, then past as they travel at vast speed. In the distance to the left Stroop points out a purple and orange cloud filled to bursting with coloured glitter, he says "If you look there you will see one of the more impressive parts of this galaxy." As they get nearer to the interstellar cloud the many stars of unwitnessed colours seem to burst open as they rush past. The edge of the smokey expanse of this nebula envelopes the ship, lighting up the control room in many mottled shades, what could be a smile almost appears on Stroops face.

The kaleidoscope of light starts to fade in passing, yet the clarity of stars kept Jack and Sue transfixed for many moments before Preep closes the wall again. "Why do you close it?" asked Jack "you're missing the view in here,"

"The beauty yes, but there are many radiations that must be kept away from entering for too long," said Preep.

"A shame," said Jack.

Sue eyed the console, "I expected there to be more buttons and lights, this looks easy."

Preep replies "Well it is mostly preprogrammed route, we have limited flexibility to survey a target dwelling, the return is entirely fixed, we just ..." Preep stops talking as Stroop gives him the glare of shut up.

"Interesting, thank you," says Sue.

Stroop gestures the pair out of the room and says "Time for some food now, to keep your strength, it is a long journey."

"Good idea," says Jack, his stomach was beginning to make quite angry noises.

Stroop enters the mess room carrying two plates of various coloured cubes, "Do not be alarmed, this food is a simulant, it is made to fit your species, there is no risk of harm to you. The texture is also simulated, the form.. not so much." Sue does not look impressed

"What happened to the meat?"

"The meat is still, frozen," Stroop hesitates to reply. Giving Preep a glare as he enters the room.

Stroop and Preep join them to eat, they too with simulated food. Prodding the cubes with their one prong fork, Jack and Sue push their food about then they try it. Though odd, the food is tasty and filling, hungry stomach's leave not a piece on the plate. They drink plain cold water from metal tankards, conversation is not forthcoming. Jack and Sue exchange glances that say 'What the hell..' While Stroop and Preep cut the cubes even tinier to fit in their narrow mouths.

Standing up Stroop says "Come, I'll show you to your sleeping quarters."

"Didn't we only just wake a little while ago?" Jack said.

"In space, we sleep when we are tired," replies Stroop.

Along the curved corridor they arrive at another identical door, and Stroop opens it. Inside sit two ornate metal beds with glass bed nobs and plush sheets. A surreal sight in such alien surroundings. To the outside of each bed a helmet just like the ones in the games room is tethered to a box. Sue notices them and says "Wait, you had these here all the time and you had us sleep in those damn chairs?!".

"We believed you were only trying it for a moment.."

"Idiots!" Sue cuts in.

They are both still tired and take little persuading to try the beds. Sue takes a hold of the nearest bed and gives it a mighty shove, to push it against the other one. She then gives Stroop a go away glare and he leaves them to undress and get some sleep.

Lying in the bed Jack wonders just how much time has passed back on earth, "John and Julie must be so worried, I wonder if there is a way to call them?, to let them know we are OK, well, I think we are OK.."

Sue is having similar thoughts too, along with trying to remember which knob does what, should opportunity arise. She mumbles to herself "As long as we get back, it will turn out fine, fine."

It didn't sound fine to Jack, Sue had too many thoughts racing, "Don't do anything silly sweetie, they have been kind so far, who knows what could happen if we make waves."

"I don't think those two are alien's finest, I've only just met them and suspect they are the Tweedle Dee and Tweedle Dum of space."

Jack sometimes forgets the exact opposite occurs whenever you try to calm someone, so just says "Good night, or good whatever it is now, sweet dreams."

5

Not known, or slipping their mind, is the fact that at these high speeds through space, there is a phenomenon known as time dilation. What was just a day on the ship, has been a week of worry back home. John and Julie's aborted dinner party and evening of frantic phoning and searching was seven long days ago. Now Jack and Sue are two more missing people, no one on earth knows where they went. John and Julie are in shock. Jenny is having trouble concentrating at work and is jabbing needles in search of a vein, searching in vein.. This sudden loss of parents is stressing Sean out more than anyone, as he is not as independent as the other offspring. Yet with his experimentation in drugs, Sean is the most likely to imagine where his folks went.

Sue and Jack are sleeping soundly, energy was low, the beds are comfy. Plus of course the mild sedative in the food helped too. In the games room Stroop and Preep have the game helmets on and are enjoying wandering the jungles of Palleen. Both are armed with a rifle and wear camouflage outfits with a bandolier hanging across their frail bodies. They tread stealthily through the undergrowth. 'Shush' Stroop gestures to Preep and they duck behind some undergrowth to look across the clearing. First just poking her scaled head out into the clearing, a beast appears, scanning her surroundings with large brown eyes. She comes forwards, more of her neck shows, then more and more, followed by her rotund body and squat legs. She is dark blue and covered with armoured scales. Swinging her serpentine neck around she eats some of the leaves in the trees adjacent to her, she chews and continues to scan around her, then lets out a squawk. Shortly two smaller heads appear.

While mother is eighteen feet high, her young are only at five feet and mottled with green over their growing frame. They waddle into the clearing and tumble and play, kicking up the dust, as clouds of tiny blue birds fly into the air letting out high pitched whistles.

In the undergrowth Stroop raises his gun and peers down the sights. Quietly he releases the safety catch and breathes steadily, waiting for the right moment. All of a sudden the mother turns in alarm at a noise behind her, this is the moment. Stroop pulls the trigger, the shot echoing through the clearing, the creatures flee back into the forest. Across the clearing from Stroop, in a bush alone, a poacher lies dead. In whistles and clicks Stroop says to Preep, "The next one is yours."

What fun is there in killing such huge beasts as this game intends. Much better to track these poachers. Several more fell to these two adventurers this day, before they returned to their duty.

6

It was a day and a half later that Jack first woke, looking at the plush covers on the bed, across to the metal scrolls of the bed frame, the glass knobs, then the cold metal walls around them. Again it came back to him that dream and reality had switched around. Looking across over the drool laden pillows, Sue is still silently sleeping. Jack goes to wake her but then thinks he should not, no one enjoys being woken up. Across on a table, their clothing lays crumpled, he holds his pullover to his nose and takes a whiff, then it registers, that it smells of dry-cleaning from the launderette. Funny how smells can bring back images so clearly, immediately his mind is taken back to earth, to picking up his suit, the same smell, many years ago, millions of miles away. He gets dressed and heads out to find Stroop.

In the mess room Stroop and Preep sit sucking up some sort of purple tentacles on their plates, they stop eating and greet Jack as he arrives around the corner. Jack goes to the box on the wall and gives it a whack to stop the light flickering, "Thank you," said Preep and he starts to clear the plates away. Stroop wipes his mouth and says "Did you and your mate sleep well? I expect you will need use of the cleaning room."

"There is a cleaning room?"

"Oh yes, of course, being clean is like being next to deity."

"Sue has not woken yet, I thought I would let her have a little more sleep, yesterday was quite full."

"You have slept for a long time, and recovered strength."

"Yes a long time, I wanted to ask you about that, is there any way to um.. to phone home? to contact our family, let them know we are ok?"

While Stroop considers the answer Sue arrives looking less than radiant, and with her shirt on inside out, "How long have we been asleep?" she asks.

Stroop considers still, then replies "There would be almost two days on your homes time pass on the ship",

"Two days?!" Sue exclaimed.

"Yes but back on your home this is a longer time passing, fourteen days."

"What!?" Sue is not best pleased with this turn of events, she spies a shape she recognises, a long rod, both she and Stroop see it in the corner of their eye, Sue in her hung over red eye, Stroop in his huge dark globe. She reaches for the rod and holds it by what looks to be the handle, Stroop looks a little alarmed but remains calm and says "Please calm, this will do you no use as the prong will only react to our command."

Sue considers, then thwacks Stroop around the side of the head with the rod, making a sound like a clean hit at the coconut shy. Jack was just taking Sue's arm when Preep jabbed them both in the behind with his freeze stick.

Stroop rubbed his head, "It was going so well, *sigh* we shall have to carry them to their quarters and confine them." Preep begins to unpick Jack's fingers from Sue's arm and takes the stick from Sue's hand. "The guests never quite accept that we have to take them back. It is just the way it must be."

They carry the heavy bodies one at a time between them, laying them on the bed. Brief disagreement, before Preep is sent in to un-freeze them and run for the door. The door slides closed and the two couples begin to spend some time separated from each other.

7

Retiring to the control room Preep and Stroop look weary, it has been a long trip, they do not enjoy stressing their subjects, but always seem to. Though these are less hysterical than most. That is why they were lent a certain freedom, while others sometimes gibbered in a room for the whole trip, a distressing sight. They sit and begin to talk in what would sound like this, if it was said in English.

"I wonder when we will have gathered enough information Stroop?"

"It may be quite a long time yet."

"We do not seem to be gathering people of importance. But we are sent to remote areas to gather our guests. It seems education is not of high regard in these places. Do you remember that one who was only concerned about missing a fight between some razorbacks and long horns?"

"Oh yes, he had seemed upset at our lack of beear."

Stroop went to another room and returned with an ice pack held against the side of his sore head.

"That is a fiery one.." said Preep, "..others have lashed out in panic before, but this seemed personal."

"That one seems to take offence at our duties, the other would rather let fate role along."

"Yes, there is possible intelligence there."

"Oh I don't think that, just wishes to not fight, even when forced into a corner, would sit and wait for fate, the other is holding intelligence within, to hide it."

"I am glad the inquisitor is facing that one and not us."

They open the viewing port to watch the stars for a while, to distract themselves from their job at hand. Often an over used phrase, this sight, this is what awesome really is.

In the quarters as Preep exits, Jack grabs at air and Sue gesticulates at the pillow, then they realise what has happened. Sue jumps up and runs to the door, banging on it, "Come back here you cowards, just sneaking about with your little sticks, put the sticks down and I'll snap your twiglet bodies!"

"Well that is hardly incentive for them to do that is it," said Jack under his breath.

"How could you just sit there, and why did I have to hit him and not you?"

"Because they are the ones who have our lives in their hands, and they have done us no harm, yet."

"Not yet, but they could be doing anything to us when we get back to their planet, and we saw the controls, the little one said it was easy, you could work out how to fly back."

"Me? just take the controls of this space ship and fly it back?, oh yes, that's going to happen.."

Sue does not appreciate the sarcasm and wishes she still had the stick in hand. Jack is not one for temper, just the occasional outburst at stubbed toes or a banged thumb. "Look," he said "They don't look happy in their work do they, maybe we could convince them that they don't need to do this job, that they could just go somewhere else and live for themselves, more chance of that than me flying a spaceship, even if they let us out of here again."

Hours pass and quiet arrives, quiet enough to hear the occasional creak of the ship's hull, though the craft's engines make less noise than the ringing of the ears. There is no feeling of movement at all, silent steel rooms traveling at a vast speed across space. Another hour passes and through a slot in the wall, a tray of food and drink arrives, Jack goes over to take it, and shouts through the slot "We really could do with using the bathroom!" A few minutes later, a bucket arrives.

8

Stroop and Preep sit at the controls of the ship, Preep presses a button and some levers appear from under the console, Stroop presses the button to open the viewing port, as Preep pulls back a lever, slowing the ship. The stars slow in their passing and a small silver globe comes into view. Slower still they approach, the globe is clearer now, some lines are marked onto it to give it some perspective, to see how near you are from it, and below it a small stalk protrudes. Preep skilfully manoeuvres the ship below the stalk and some sound is heard rumbling above as lights are checked and clamps are locked.

Stroop stands up and clicks "Would you like anything from the shop?"
"Just a Starrbur if they have one."
"At this fuelling price, nourishment should be free."

Stroop takes his shoulder bag from a hook and walks through the corridor to the lift. Travelling up the narrow tube into the service station. Inside the station there is a small array of coloured drinks and brightly wrapped snacks of all kinds. At the end of an isle a small desk sits, on the desk a glass screen protects the keeper at the desk. A large grey blob of a being with a face incapable of joy sits, "Number please?" he enquires,

"There is only one fuel bay."
"Which number please," he repeats,

"One?"

Stroop puts his credit disc into the slot and waits for the green light. All around the universe, in every galaxy, green is the yes of colours.

"Oh I misremember, also a Starrbur, and a Chocachoo." Stroop again waits for the green light. Then leaves the keeper to his thoughts.

Returning to the control room he hands Preep his Starrbur, "I am sure these were of higher proportion before," he grumbles, as he disengages from the station and accelerates the ship away.

Stroop and Preep enter Jack and Sue's quarters, each carrying a chair in one hand and a prod in the other. They look somewhat like anaemic lion tamers. They take a seat in their chairs, keeping hold of their freeze prods. Stroop takes a breath and says "Let us start again, I am Stroop and this is Preep, we are from Ool, we are charged with collection of higher beings for assessment, and your names are?" Preep looks across to Stroop a little nervously, unsure of this plan to befriend the guests. Jack and Sue shuffle forwards to sit at the end of the bed, eyeing the prods carefully, Jack now puts his plan into action. "I am Jack and this is my wife Sue, from earth.., you know you do not really have to take us back to your planet, you could just take us home and disappear, there must be so many planets, where no one would ever find you, no more orders, no more of this old ship." He forces a hopeful smile.

"Oh you are coming back with us, that is certain, Jack," said Stroop, "You said earlier of sending message to people you left, for their heart? You have a communicator?"

Jack continues an impotent plea "Don't be too hasty, there is always choice..", Sue interjects, "You were trying to phone home Jack? I have a phone in the car, it will still have battery, I only turn it on to phone out."

Sue is trying hard to stay on the plan for now, as the alternative is not great, even for the most frustrated abductee, at least on earth there would be somewhere to escape to.

"We shall search your car. If a communicator is found, we shall send confirmation of your life to your predetermined destination, but we must not be known." They then get up to leave. There is temptation, but Sue just hands Preep the half full bucket for emptying.

Stroop locks the door behind him and turns to Preep, "Search their vehicle and see if there is a suitable communicator, we can maybe build a bridge to help calm."

9

Entering the hanger Preep finds Betsy sitting where she was abandoned days ago. The front doors still open, he did not fail to see the parallels between this old car and their ship. Still going, long after their peers have been sent back to their maker. He pokes and prods at the handles of the doors, taking in how the mechanisms work. Walking around the back he notes the door shut lines and searches for a button of entry, button found and pressed the boot opens a little. Preep stands back and waits, before approaching and lifting it up. Inside various things are piled, plaid blankets, tool boxes, bags and a package of bright colour wrapped in a gold bow.

All is searched and the present is opened, revealing a long striped ribbon of indeterminate use. A rusty tool set is scattered and blankets are unfolded. No communicator is found. Over the back seat Preep spies a bag and reaches over to retrieve it, tipping it empty into the back of the car. All manner of things spill out, including the phone.

He takes the phone back to his bench, in his workshop, and begins to take it apart to analyse it's construction. Stroop enters and looks over Preeps shoulder, "They told us truth of having a communicator?"

"Yes, although this will need much adjustment, this is inadequate to send a signal to anywhere much further than a shouts travel. But there is means to location and it will be possible to send to the saved coordinates."

"Do so, I shall think how to explain absence."

In the secured quarters, Sue and Jack are enjoying some cake after hearing that their family will be getting to know that they are in fact still alive and well and will be returning in a month or so. A small piece of reassurance that they are not adrift entirely.

Back on earth, in a large house with a double garage, in a spacious room with plush furnishings of oak, John sits at the dining table, sitting opposite his wife Julie. They are both finishing eating spaghetti bolognese, John mopping up the sauce with some bread. Julie wipes the sauce from baby Jack's face. The phone starts to ring.

In the early days of Jack and Sue's absence, there were many calls back and forth. The police were very active, neighbours searched, John even made an appearance on local television to appeal for information. There were many reassurances, but no information was forthcoming. Of course there was the occasional silly story, but no real lead as to where his parents had disappeared to. It had been five weeks since they went missing and the phone had stopped ringing this last week, people had run out of assurances and pats on the shoulder, now they left them to some peace and quiet. So when the phone rang, it came as a bolt out of the blue.

John gets up and presses the green button on the phone, holds it to his ear, as Julie starts to load the dishwasher. "Hello?" Some loud crackling makes him wince, then a thin voice asks "Am I speaking to John Shaw?"

"Yes, I am John Shaw, who is this?"

"I am… Paul, I am to inform you that your parents are safe and well, and will be back in approximately two months more."

"This is not funny, how would you feel if your parents died? What do you get out of this sick joke?"

"There is no falseness, I assure you, we just have a few tests to do, then they will return."

"OK then suppose this is true, let me speak to my father"

"Very well, but a short time, we must not share too much."

A few crackles and a high pitched squeal makes John move the receiver from his ear once more. Then he hears his mum Sue, "Hello sweetheart how are you?"

"Where did I go to school?"

"What?.. erm.. Somerfield high school."

"Where have you been?! We've been worried sick!"

"It's a long stor…"

Her voice fades and the thin voice returns, "We apologise for inconvenience, your guardians will be back in due time.. thank you." Then the receiver clicks and they are gone.

"Hello hello?" He tries to redial but the number is unavailable.

So now he knows his parents are alive. Just being experimented on by unknown terrorists. He re-runs the phone call in his head. He thinks of the things he should have said, should have asked. Then relays all to Julie and finally they have a much needed hug.

10

On board the ship, tearing through space, ever nearer their destination, the planet Knool. All four are sat around the mess table, Stroop hands the phone back to Preep and says "Now they do know that you are going to return."
Sue has mixed feelings, "You didn't have to cut me off, I just wanted to know how they were.."

Jack says "Thank you, it was good of you."

"We could not risk any longer communication."
Jack is in inquisitive mood and asks "I was wondering, with your sticks to freeze your abductees.."

"Guests," Stroop interrupts.

"To freeze your guests.. why do you not just freeze us for the whole journey? Would it not be easier?" Stroop thinks for a while, then says "Most often our guests are not in any condition to see what is happening, most are distressed, but we agree, I and Preep, that the smallest chance to see joy in a guest, when they see what is out here, beyond their species capacity, to see those eyes, it is worth some small trouble."

Preep goes and locks the phone away, returning to the galley to finish preparing some food. Before final preparations for the approach to the security stop off at Sool.

Through the viewport a tangerine haze flows into the control room. The luminous planet of Sool fills the window. Even from thousands of miles up here, the planet looks industrious and unnatural. The console's communicator crackles into life and some clicks and whistles are heard. Stroop replies, a routine as ordinary as checking into an airport terminal. Though guilt is always there to be felt, whether innocent or not. Stroop nods to Preep and they begin their descent.

No ship may pass through this sector without checking in at Sool. No lethal weaponry is permitted in this sector, though the search is swift, it must take place on the surface of the planet. An inconvenience, but none wish to risk being blown to bits for the non compliance of peace.

The ship begins to shudder when they enter the atmosphere, little ant trails of ships can be seen down below, many thousands of ships making their way along the set routes, soon this ship too joins a queue.

Jack is on the beach as he feels the sand beneath him shudder, while the sea sits as still as ever, the contrast from his real and virtual body is dealing Jack's brain a hazy time. He removes the helmet and sets it down, then leaves the games room and goes to find Sue. He finds her in the quarters, doing a word search from one of the puzzle books recovered from Betsy. "Did you feel that earlier? It's never done that before."

"They said they were preparing for something, maybe this old heap is low on fuel again?"

"I'll go see what they are up to."

In the control room he finds Preep is concentrating on adjusting some controls, while Stroop chatters over the communicator.

Through the window a long queue of ships of all shapes and sizes strings down to infinity way down to the surface of this massive orange planet. In appearance it is nearest Mars, but painted in iridescent hues. The nearest ship ahead is a massive hulk of a thing with arms reaching out with empty pylons, looking like a neutered gunship, Preep keeps a safe distance anyway.

Jack watches the goings on over his crew's shoulders. Strange there are so many ships, it seemed the universe was so sparse not long ago, no doubt once done, all will disperse to nothingness again, like a border crossing in infinity, he thought.

An hour later and the planet is nearer, the parked ships can be seen in the distance. Huge cannons face into space, to maintain the peace. Stroop leaves the control room, he is off to ensure that all is tidy, to get this check over with quickly.

On returning to the control room he meets Sue on the way, "We will soon be boarded for a check, to ascertain that we are not bearing lethal arms. If you wish, you and Jack may leave the ship to observe the new land. Wear a hat and shoes, the temperature is much above what you are used to."

"But we'll die out there without some sort of mask, we can't breath alien air?"

"Oh it is the same as earth air. This is why so few planets are populated, they all need air for us to breath."

"Makes sense."

Finally it is their turn to land for inspection. Distant clanks and whirs are heard as the landing gear extends from the underbelly, a cloud of orange sparkling dust is scattered as the craft settles. "If you would follow please," says Stroop, as Preep shuts the craft down for a while. Hats rest on Jack and Sue's heads, though as ever, they are intended for a larger head, but needs must. They walk down a long landing ramp, so long due to the ridiculous long legs jutting from under the saucer. The air is very hot but there is very little humidity. The planet was long ago turned over to industry, all nature gone, all provisions for the living here being created artificially, including the air. But there is no escaping the fact that this planet is nearer it's sun, so the heat remains.

Turning around, Sue looks at the outside of their prison for the first time since being in the car. It is a vast disc with no markings and no lights, no nozzles nor engines to be seen. Ahead Stroop meets one of the inspectors, he speaks in grunts to the short green alien, not in disrespect, the grunts are their language.

The two inspectors are around four feet tall and have tiny dark eyes, a crust of scales reside atop their head and they wear an orange suit, which looks like it is made entirely of hoses. In their long spindly hands they hold note books. Stroop and Preep can only watch them waddle up the ramp and hope they pass inspection.

Sue is really starting to feel the heat, the sweat dripping down her back. She lifts the over-size sun hat to wipe her brow with her sleeve. Across from the saucer, another ship is being attended to. More of the same inspectors, talking to two tall people. From a distance they look human. On closer inspection the proportions are off and their faces appear to be stretched hollywood tight against their skull.

From where Sue is standing it seems like they sound of a familiar tongue. So she walks over to find out a little more. Clearly the tall owners of an elegant white ship are not in agreement with the inspectors. Sadly for Sue, she finds they are not speaking her language. There are similar sounds but in a different order. They give off a charismatic air, that they could charm the birds from the trees. But they are having trouble penetrating the inspectors unimaginative mind. Sue approaches and interrupts the nearest tall stranger, "Could you help us please? We are being abducted and taken to do God knows what on a strange planet." They both stop and stared down, and up at Sue, then the tall man speaks in fine English. "Oh yes, you are from Earth, travelling with Stroop, a fine fellow, you are in safe hands, and you will find Knool a charming place, it is the most beautiful of their planets, have a wonderful time."

He then turns and continues his conversation with the inspector. Sue doesn't know whether to feel offended or reassured, but is certainly struck dumb. Jack is over by a very odd looking ship with pipes and cogs protruding everywhere, he gestures and shouts for Sue to come over. "Look at this? It's incredible isn't it? You can't see anything on our ship, but this one is like an open Swiss watch, have you ever seen anything so beautiful?" Jack was letting his mind forget about the possible future, the worry of home and just letting it enjoy for a bit. Sue for this moment, synced with this feeling, to enjoyed his joy.

Before the tall ones have finished their argument, the inspectors return from out of the saucer, they hold their cards close to their chest, approaching Stroop with the results of inspection. It seems to Sue that they are nodding agreement, but she is unsure whether she wants a pass or not. If they fail then what? Perhaps lasers to be torn out, and there will to be a long wait. Or will they just be turned back, forced to take us back home? Hopes rise in one moment, then one moment later, Stroop is gesturing them over. Time to get back into the ship.

11

A welcome waft of refreshing cold air hits them as they enter the ship, away from the furnace outside, Preep restarts the systems, and warms them through for some moments, till they are ready to pull up and away, leaving the bright tangerine orb and it's endless queues of ships far behind, back into the lonely void of space.

The ship feels like it is now silently gliding again. Though it is tearing through space at a speed that is still just theory for the scientists of Earth. Preep and Jack sit finishing their food, while Stroop watches the gauges in the control room and Sue visits the bathroom. Jack asks "What will they ask us when we arrive at umm, Nool isn't it?"

"Knool.. It is not for us to tell you what you may be asked. No one has ever died in questioning, if that is a worry for you. Our guests have always returned, although we will not be returning you."

"No death, good to hear, You won't be returning us?"

"The return is left to faster ships, speed in exchange for having to release you on the ground. [A sight the people of Earth often mistaken for shooting stars] The new ships have no capacity for a lift beam."

"That would be a shame, you have been good to us, I hope the other crew are as kind." Pausing, then adds "That planet we went to, so many different aliens, the universe is a busier place than I ever thought."

"You are very sheltered, but you were right, the universe is mostly empty, if the universe were your planet, all of life would be just a speck on the tip of this finger." Preep inadvertently gives Jack the finger. So Jack casually tells of some of Earth's trivia "On earth that is a sign of disrespect, to raise your middle finger like that."

"Perhaps like showing teeth in our culture?"

"I don't know, maybe. Would someone get angry when they did that?"

"Yes, on occasion, though violent act is no longer popular."

"Haha, out of fashion to be violent?! Now there is an answer, to make violence uncool."

Sue comes back into the mess room and takes a seat, "I can't get used to that wash room, standing there and feeling my skin creep, waiting for a light to go off, are you sure it's safe?"

"Oh quite safe of course" says Preep, "A simple derma freshening device."

"Damn creepy," says Sue.

Jack stacks the plates and pushes them to the end of the table "I learned that violence is unfashionable on Knool, and we will be there in another week." Sue laughs

"Maybe we can bring it back into fashion there."

Preep lets this go, instead answering Jack "Yes. Maybe one day earlier if we are spotted earlier. If they wish to draw us on the pattern beam for the last part of the journey."

12

Between Sue and Jack there is talk of returning to the games room to take some time on the beach again. Or perhaps a walk in the woods. But these thoughts are cut short when an alarm sounds. Twittering noises shake their eardrums and red lights flash, Preep rushes off to the control room to see what is going on. "Pirates," clicks Stroop. Lights flash on the console and a ship appears on a screen.

The pirates know that this whole sector is unarmed, though they are also unarmed for the same reason. It is thought they prey on the forgetful. They hope the intended victims will surrender before they remember there is nothing the pirates can do if they do not surrender.

Of course there is sheer size that can come into effect, if they happen to have a legal grappling claw, or if they can simply take the other ship into the larger ship's hangar.

This ship, as it appears on the screen does not bring any worry to Stroop. It is small and they are living on wishful thinking if they feel they can capture such a large saucer.

Jack leans in between the seats "Do we have trouble?"

"Just pirates, they are harmless" replies Stroop.

Sue leans on the door frame and says "First time I've heard of a harmless pirate. How do you know they are pirates?" Preep presses a button, a close up picture of the pirate's ship appears "They send a marker from this mast. They hope to scare the unwary into foolishness."

Preep turns to Stroop and discusses a course of action, opens up the fine controls of the ship and hunkers down to concentrate. Stroop opens the viewing port then turns to Jack, "To attempt to prevent further trouble for the moment from these pirates, Preep is going to attempt to disable the signal."

Preep concentrates, while the other three watch through the view port. It is always a pleasure to see out of the view port, even though they spend their day amongst the stars, they get little time to see them. They are shining crystal clear in all colours, such is the ship's velocity, many are passing by, though millions of miles away.

The pirate ship comes into view, it is attempting to match the speed of the inbound saucer, a blinking speck in the distance at first, but Preep must maintain high speed if his plan is to work, "Are you going to jam their signal?" Jack asks. But no reply, Preep keeps his attention on the pirate ship, getting closer at a vast rate now, it is a dark tangle of aerials and jutting pylons, "You're going to hit it!" Sue exclaims. All hold their breath as Preep guides the controls, closer, closer, the ship is suddenly filling the view port, a Clunk! is heard reverberating through the hull then the ship is gone, far behind.

"They will no longer manage to lure victims, without their aerial," says Stroop, and places his hand on Preeps shoulder.

13

Far behind, Earth the beautifully swirled marble, gently carousels. Way down on the surface the rain is hammering against Jenny's kitchen window. She is checking her Facebook status. What she read on Sean's page has got more and more worrying and now there is nothing, and he is not answering messages, nor the phone, he has been un-anchored, adrift for a while now.

Pamela comes in from work and kisses Jenny on the forehead, "Still no word from Sean?" Pamela asks. Jenny puts her arm around Pamela's waist, "No, nothing, I'm going to go see how he is."

"I'll come with you, give me a minute to freshen up."

Fifteen minutes later they run through the rain to climb into Jenny's little beaten up hatchback and head over to Sean's apartment. It is pitch black, but no stars to see, as the heavy rain sees to that. The wipers are struggling to keep up with the clouds tears, the drains are struggling to cope too and the water is starting to get deep at the bottom of the hill. But the old faithful car makes it up the hill to Sean's place.

Weeds frame the soaked paving slabs and graffiti shines on the fence. They climb the slick iron steps and get into the building out of the rain, up the stairs to the right, Sean's door is closed, Jenny knocks, "Sean Sean! are you in there? No trouble, we just want to know you're OK." She reaches in her pocket, gets out the key and pushes it into the lock.

The door is caught with the security chain. These chains are designed to stop a thief, but not a worried sister. In two shoulder barges Jenny tears the screws from the rotten wood.

"Phone the ambulance Pam," she cries, as she rushes to Sean's side. He is curled on the bed, almost peacefully. The evidence is sat on the table. Jenny checks Sean for vital signs, but Sean left here several hours ago. Pamela never did call, it was in the stars. There was nothing to do but for Jenny to pour her grief out onto Pamela's shoulder.

In the saucer's hanger, Jack is admiring his car Betsy. He runs his hand along the doors and imagines some road beneath the tyres, rather than the metal. He opens the drivers door and takes a sit in the seat and looks across the dashboard, imagining blue sky through the windshield. He glances down to the console, to the radio, "I haven't heard music for so long. I wonder.." He turns the ignition key, but nothing. The courtesy lights have drained the battery. In ordinary times, we imagine the extraordinary, and here in extraordinary times, Jack longs for the ordinary.

He wiggles the steering wheel from side to side and uses his imagination for a bit, until Preep peeks around the corner wondering what the squeaking noise is, and Jack, embarrassed, stops. "Just reminiscing," he says as he climbs out.

Sue is in the sleeping quarters, "What's wrong with books?" she says to Stroop, "We have many books, just not physical books, there are whole libraries in the machine."

He places the helmet device on Sue's head and adjusts it. She lays back, wrenching the cord out of the socket, "Maybe a little nearer to the box," says Stroop.

Opening her eyes Sue is standing on a marble floor in a huge library, two carved oak staircases spiral up each side of her, up to the landing. Book cases stand proudly in rows reaching over twenty feet high. Ladders are hung from brass rails to reach the higher volumes. Above the cases, way up above, seemingly touching the sky, a vaulted glass ceiling of many stained glasses, lighting the space in bright hues. Sue climbs the stairs feeling the grain of the balustrade beneath her fingers, the stairs creak and the familiar musky smell of thousands of books fills her nostrils.

As she gets to the top of the stairs, she spies through the endlessly tall cases some seating, and beyond the seating, colossal arched windows frame greenery, but they are too far away to tell exactly what is out there for now.

To the right there is a small desk and Sue only just notices a librarian quietly sitting at the desk, hunkered down with his head in a book. He is old and wizened, what is left of his hair is wispy and grey and he is wearing round glasses at the tip of his nose. Sue approaches him and asks "Excuse me, whereabouts is your crime section?" The Librarian places his book down and eyes Sue up and down, "Just over there on the left and right of case three, anything in particular you are looking for?" Sue pauses, then says in sarcastic flair, "Thank you, no don't you worry, you get back to your book, I'll just go browse." The momentarily distracted librarian disappears back into his book.

Sue looks at the hundreds of titles scrolling past her eyes as she walks down isle three. They all seem recognisable. Surely these all can't have been printed, not all real she thinks to herself. After an hour of flicking through many many books, every one she pulls out bears words, and all are well thumbed. Sue takes an intriguing looking title and goes to sit down. Nearer the rear of the library she can see through the widows properly.

She takes a seat and watches as outside a brachiosaurus browses the leaves of the mighty coniferous trees in the expansive jungle garden. Yes she thinks, this might be better than taking some books with you. She sits and gets lost in her book, time slips past easily as she reads her book right through from cover to cover.

14

Preep and Stroop are sitting at the controls when they feel a jolt. They have been registered in the distance, and though a little late, the pattern beam is drawing them in to Knool.

Jack wanders into the control room, "What was the turbulence about?" Stroop finishes correcting some controls and turns to Jack "We have been engaged by Knool and will be arriving in half a day."

"So we will soon be saying goodbye to you?"

"Yes, this adventure will end, and another will start."

"If I don't get to talk to you again, thank you Stroop."

Back on earth the leaves are starting to turn copper as autumn begins to paint it's colours, there is a chill in the air, but the rain is just about holding off. John watches the casket being lowered into the grave. He and Jenny's families are there, though Sean's friends were not welcome nor invited, not that they cared to attend. One unrecognised young lady is in attendance keeping her distance away from the rest, it is hard to tell if she is upset or not at this distance, she leaves before the family disperses. Julie is answering her phone, the baby sitter has bad timing to ask where baby Jack's favourite toy might be. She impatiently says "It's definitely in the cot, maybe under the blanket..," then shuts off the phone.

Thoughts drift to those not here, the fond memories, the open-endedness, if it is an ending or just a pause. Jenny carries a wreath back to the car, as they all drive off to honour Sean with drinks and a meal.

The saucer is hurtling towards a bright green and blue orb, as Earth, yet not quite. Continents are larger and seas less so, with little cloud to be seen. Green and blue both tipped in iridescent direction on the colour scale, giving Knool a tie dye appearance. They appear to be about to arrive at the centre of Knool like a dart into a board, but now there is a slowing sensation and the ship begins to tremble.

As the saucer hits the atmosphere Stroop temporarily closes the viewing window. The ship shudders and some things are heard to be falling off the mess table. Always some things forgotten. Stroop turns to his guests "My apologies, the ship does not compensate for the pattern beam well." Jack is enjoying the excitement "No problem, it's good to feel we are really moving for a change." Sue is a little quiet and looking a touch pale.

Stroop says to Sue "Do not worry, we will soon be into the atmosphere, normality will resume."

As promised the serene ride returns and Stroop re-opens the viewing port, revealing a turquoise sky bearing wispy clouds. Below, a carpet of marble flat sea flashes beneath the ship.

In the hazy distance a shoreline emerges, again green, so green this planet, completely unexpected. Both Jack and Sue look out in amazement, they were expecting metal and industry and smog, a planet seeking a place to escape to. But instead they find this distant paradise, perhaps a false paradise.

Now the first buildings are seen. Not sky scraping ones like the cities of earth, they are low, or at least seem low from up here. They hug the ground and are made up of what looks like saucers and sails, looking like abandoned boats in the woods.

The ship flies low and slows on it's final approach, nearly brushing the tall trees, disturbing the colourful flying creatures in the upper boughs. Bright coloured wings flicker as they flee.

A pristine landing platform is ready to receive the craft. Two other ships either side of the vacant spot for this saucer, which now looks more old and rundown than ever. The other two ships sparkle in white with green accents, they ooze pure speed, while not moving one inch. Preep extends the landing gear and double checks the pattern beam is still engaged.

The whole ship seems to sigh as it settles down, finally home again.

15

Stroop turns to Sue and Jack, "Time for us to part, thank you, you have made the time mostly pleasant" Jack unexpectedly attempts a hug, alarming the poor alien, instead he settles for an awkward half wave. Sue says "Thank you, you could have been worse" then follows Preep to the exit ramp.

At the end of the ramp a tall figure waits to greet them, he is of the same species it seems as their hosts, yet his head is smaller, more in line with human proportion. Different also from their saucer crew, as he is wearing clothing. A loose white top with gold accents and green trousers, he gives a half smile, "Welcome to Knool, I am Roomp, I hope your journey was pleasant, please follow me, we have refreshment, I will then introduce you to the inquisitor".

Jack reciprocates a similar smile "Pleased to meet you, I am Jack and this is Sue". They follow Roomp along the gantry to the building, glancing across to see Stroop and Preep chatting to what looks like an engineer. They are discussing how a small dent on the left side of the disc occurred.

Sue looks over the side of the gantry, and regrets it immediately in a wobble of vertigo. The ground is nowhere to be seen. Tree trunks stretch to infinity down below, with grey bark and leaves in pastel greens. The turquoise sky is starting to give them a headache until Roomp remembers to give them cancelling glasses, a little too late, as they are now entering the building.

Inside it is hard to tell if this was inspired by car showrooms or if car showrooms were inspired by the rooms of Knool. All is open, clean and well lit. "Please, come," Roomp says, as he guides them through a round tunnel hallway with curved glass. Through which they can see the trees and catch a glimpse of one of the coloured birds. On closer inspection, they got the scale all wrong first time they spotted them on the flight in. Though feathered like a rainbow macaw, they must be around six feet tall, and appear to be gripping the branches with four muscular arms. Sue catches a glimpse of the giant bird launching off a branch down into the depths of the forest.

At the end of the tunnel a room is set with many chairs around a rectangular table. The table is laden with familiar looking food, familiar from the ship, not home, all produced by machine, but this food is produced with beauty on a plate in mind. Roomp asks "Please, sit, eat, drink." All three take a seat, Sue and Jack admire the setting. The walls are allowed a little decoration here, it makes the base a little more homely. Some orange and gold accents drape on the walls and round monitors show various scenes of Knool, a waterfall, a rocky shore and some of what looks like young Knoolians playing in looped footage. Instead of very functional hidden lighting, the lighting here is more extravagant, large fanned shells produce a strong natural light.

Sue gets to the point, "So, when do we get asked questions so we can leave?" Jack is more inclined to take in as much as possible "Now hold on Sue, we only just got here, did you see those little black birds earlier? They were amazing, they made those starling murmurations look like amateurs. Darting about, flashing colour under their wings, wonderful."

Roomp takes in both views, "The inquisitor will be here momentarily. Yes there is no hurry, as Jack here says, there is much to enjoy." Sue gives a look to Jack "It looks very dangerous out there to me," she says. Roomp replies, "Oh no, there is no chance of harm to you at all, the Ilena are protected from the wild, and the wild protected from Ilena." Jack and Sue look a little confused, so Roomp adds "Ilena is us, as you are human." He starts to eat between giving Jack and Sue a brief description of Ilenaian history. "We began on Ool, we were like many races, destructive and selfish, we soon were too much for one place. Through advancements we explored and found Knool, here we put into practice our lessons learned, and yes, Ool is recovering also." Sue looks a little horrified that maybe her fears all along were correct, "So you are just searching for more planets to conquer?" Roomp aghast "Oh no, we are completely sustained here, it is quite the opposite."

The sun is starting to set on Knool, both Jack and Sue take some pride in Knool's smaller sun not being quite the display of earth's at sunset, bright green dims to khaki as it sinks over the horizon. With the sun setting, the view from the window gathers a more menacing appearance as the trees begin to whip back and forth as the wind rises, the clouds build and pour across the sky appearing like a time lapse video. Though well insulated in this building, they can still hear the wind whistle. Faint vibrations are felt from the stronger gusts. Jack says "It really is like night and day with this weather change.." An imaginary tumbleweed tumbles.

The food finished with, they try the drink, an unusual but sweet beverage, with a slight kick. "Is this alcoholic?" says Jack to Roomp, "alcoholic? You know, is this made to make your head, you know, swim?"

"Oh no no, just a slight addition, for interest."

Jack finishes the drink and encourages Sue "Try it, it's good stuff." Sue gives it a wary sniff.

"I am fine with water thanks." She turns to Roomp and asks "Do you have a bathroom?"

"Oh yes, this way thank you."

He leads them down a hall to the smallest room, inside there are again funnels sprouting from the floor, though decorated with painted leaves, even the luxury of a mop on a stick.

When Sue and Jack return to the dining room, they find two huge sentinels have arrived, guarding the entrance. They stand around seven feet high and have long dark hair spouting from their heads hanging down to their waists. What can be seen of their faces is of dark green complexion, they are in a military like uniform and hold long staffs. It seems they have been told of Jack and Sue's arrival and silently let them pass to retake their seats in the dining room. Just as they do Roomp returns with a colleague, though not as tall as the sentinels and with shorter hair, he has the same complexion, and a wide mouth with a welcoming smile. Roomp introduces him, "Jack, Sue, this is Jax, your prescribed inquisitor."

Jax strides forward offering his hand to both Jack and Sue "Wonderful to meet you, Stroop tells me much of you. The food is good? And the drink?" Jack is taken with the enthusiasm. "Yes thank you, the drink was delicious, and the food too. It is very beautiful here, but the weather, the weather is crazy."

"Haha, yes, the nights here are rather hard, better to be in here than out there. Please follow me, it is time for you to rest, I shall show you to your quarters." Sue is not quite so enthusiastic, "No questions now?"

"Oh no, it is too late for that tonight, have some rest, we will enjoy tomorrow fully with rest."

So Jack and Sue are led to a plush and welcoming room with a skylight, through which they can just about see the clouds shooting past in the dark. Two beds sit side by side. They are carved of unknown horn and are looking more than welcoming for two tired travellers.

16

Panning back to earth, across the stars, the once keen leaves have left their branches and are chasing each other around the park at the whim of the wind. On a park bench Jenny and Pamela sit together and watch the leafy dance. Their breath forms twin clouds as it hits the chill air. They have been together for over a year and never shown a hint that there was ever going to be a time that either would seek another. Pamela nervously reaches into her pocket and retrieves a small box, an offer to Jenny, commitment forever, in the box a question, the answer is yes.

The turquoise haze filters through the skylight as daytime arrives on Knool. They have slept well, but always do, they could fall fast asleep on a broken bicycle. Sue wakes first and notes that Jack's beard is starting to fill, and also notes that she is not that disappointed. On a table at the end of the bed some clothing lies. A pair of tunics and some over size trousers with a cord tie at the waist. Sue considers wearing her clothes yet again, but then opts to try these for size. They fit surprisingly well, she only wishes there was a bra, as hers has developed a life of it's own. Off she walks to the bathroom, uses the facilities and washes without water again. It even surprises Sue how normal it is beginning to feel, like the last the mid stretch of a hotel stay, routine is sought out by the mind.

As she returns to the bedroom Jack is awake and rolling up the new trousers on his under size legs.

"Not bad eh?" says Jack as he ties the cord in a knot.

"Could be worse, let's go see what they have planned for breakfast."

The guards are still standing at the entrance of the dining room in menacing reassurance. Sue wonders if she might have some fun with them, but thinks better of it, only the antagonist looks foolish when one fools with a sentry. So they sit and nibble at the buffet on the table and drink a little water.

Jax bounds in looking full of enthusiasm, "Ah, I see you made use of the nightwear! Good to see you feel more comfortable. We will soon be seeing something that I hope you will find fun, I'll be back momentarily." Then out again he hurries. Roomp comes in moments later holding some clothing, similar style to the pyjamas, yet heavier and better fitting, in chocolate brown and gold. His assistant offers some sandals to try, both Sue and Jack are disconcerted by the self tightening straps on them, but they are comfortable. Jax returns with a small notepad like device. "OK, are we ready? follow me, transport is waiting." They both hurry after the energetic Jax. Sue asks "Are you not asking questions?" Jax waves his hand "No no, later later."

They return to the platform where they landed. One large elegant ship remains. The saucer is gone and a small sleek craft sits alongside the large one, a long narrow ramp is lying out under the nose of the craft, like a tongue.

The Ilena pilot beckons them over. Sue, Jack, Roomp and Jax board with the pilot.

In the passenger compartment the chairs sit opposing one another with tables between. No tiny portholes here, the whole of each side of the craft is window, allowing a full view of the scenery. They settle down into the seats and the pilot guides the craft into the air and sweeps around and up.

Through the window the forest falls away, then nears again as the pilot allows some flamboyance in his path, sweeping along at the tree tops he disturbs the birds, before arriving at the coastline, sharply turning to follow the rocky coast. Roomp suddenly starts remembering something, and says "Your glasses! Here, put these on." Sue takes them and hands one pair across to Jack. Jax has his nose against the glass watching the waves sweep past. "Did you see that!? Something big just leapt." Jack joins him in eyeing the sea for movement but he seems to have hexed the fish spotting. Sue is looking out of the other window and spies several large blue creatures sunning themselves on the rocks.

The forest is thinning now, giving way to wetlands, as the rocks no longer protect the land. An endless moss now fills one window and the sea remains on the other side. They turn their attention away from the windows. Sue asks Jax "Where are we going to anyway, a diner?" Jax presses a button on the table and a map appears. He scrolls across then points to a twisting track in holographic form, "Right here, to see the races, a place of gambling." Sue looks shocked "Gambling? In so called advanced society? Gambling sucks all the money from the desperate."

Roomp interjects "Only those who are able may gamble, it is a fun thing."

"Fun for the house," said Sue.

A few trees begin to reappear in the window, the moss giving way to forest again and the ship begins to slow. First banking out to sea, then turning back towards land. A ribbon of track lies in amongst the trees below them. A massive mesh parking cube sits next to the forest, full of various ships. Alongside, three platforms sit in a row. The ship spirals down and lands on the centre platform, "Off we go," says Jax and they all head down the ramp into the melee of people of all worlds heading towards the races.

Jack looks back to watch the ship being automatically valet parked into the cage and shakes his head in amazement.

17

Jax produces a stick from his pocket and presses a button, unfurling a bright red flat canopy over his head. He says "It is shade from sun, and also you can find me if you get lost." The crowds are starting to funnel to the entrance now and progress is slow. Sue says "Bit of a coincidence this happening as soon as we arrive isn't it?" Jax laughs "Oh, this happens every day. Though not the same crowd no."

Looking around it seems that there are families recognisable in the crowd. Mini versions of their parents walk along in their idiosyncratic way. Some smaller children are holding hands to keep in touch in the throng. Nearer the entrance large arches light up green as each person passes through, across to the right an arch lights red and a small mouse like being is pulled aside to explain why this would occur. He looks surprised, he waves to his family through the arch waiting for him.

Roomp hands Sue and Jack a card each and they pass through an arch. It lights green and they walk onwards. Sue looks around and sees a familiar sight, she says "Right, first things first, I need the loo."

Jack tuts "Why didn't you go before we left?"

"I did go before we left." Then she asks Roomp "Which is the ladies?"

"The ladies? Do ladies deposit differently on your planet? the same place, sex or species." So she goes and joins what looks like the shortest queue, behind a rotund hairy alien, shuffling impatiently from foot to foot.

So not to lose touch, not to get lost, the other three join the rest of the bathroom lurkers. Jack asks Jax "On board the saucer, Sue said there are huge libraries in the game machine, all books of earth, so what could we possibly tell you here that are not in those books already?" Jax ponders a moment then says "We may have much knowledge there in those machines, but the machine reads the users thought too, to fill in some gaps, and many books may have been stored, but not all have been read, it is hard to judge a word and an action, which is real, which is story? Also direct knowledge is not always the goal, sometimes a feeling is truer than a book." Sue re-emerges from the loo a little flustered and says "Best hold it in Jack."

Just around the corner nearer the track a large row of booths stretches two hundred feet long, each one has a screen and eight coloured buttons, simplicity itself. Just eight runners each with their colour. The turnover is fast and there are so many booths that there is no queueing, Jax demonstrates. He pushes the card in, presses for race seven, pushes a blue button and then the card comes out again. Jack picks green, Sue picks red, Roomp declines to bet.

Now they have placed their bets, it's time to go see the racers. Walking past eateries and beautiful topiary borders they approach bunches of round glass pods, like an enormous bunch of crystal grapes. Each one is boarded by around six people, then sweeps up into the air to gain a good view of the races.

As one after the other globe swings way up into the air, Sue gets more and more nervous of this possibility "We're not going up there are we?" Jax reassures Sue "It is a fine way to see, and very safe, you will see nothing from down here." Jack knows that he will miss out too if he doesn't convince Sue it is OK, "Don't worry you can't fall, look they are all sealed up, safe in a ball."

"Flung up into the air like a kamikaze hamster," says Sue.

Soon they are the next to board and Sue takes a deep breath and takes a step forward into the pod, Jack gives her a smile and a squeeze, which she shrugs off and holds the hand rail. Her knuckles turn white, the door closes and the bubble sweeps into the sky in one smooth motion.

From up in the air they can see the long ribbon of track sweep and curve as a roller coaster. Below them directly is the start line, six racing darts sit on the line. The scale now realised as the last two are placed there by two heavy set beings carrying them under their arms like a canoe, the vehicles are only around five feet long. "Oh, they are radio control cars," says Jack, but then he sees a canopy open and a tiny pilot climbs aboard with helmet in hand, barely two feet high and long of limb in skin tight racing suit. The pilot wriggles into the race dart and the canopy seals him in.

Now all eight racers sit hovering just above the surface of the track, alongside the track are dots on a signal board, indicating the race number, to allow for every language to see which race is being run. This one being number four. The race they have a bet on being number seven, but they all pick a colour in this race anyway. Jack picks blue as the dart looks shiny and brand new, Jax picks red as it is battered and old, so knows the circuit well.

A tweeting sound announces the time to clear the track. So the handlers collect with their small boxes of tools, leaving the circuit to the purposeful looking darts. In the pod a commentary of unknown language begins over hidden speaker, Roomp flicks through the language options and says "Sorry, no human languages are options."

"Don't worry," says Jack "Commentators are all the same, only there to state the obvious."

The darts begin to hum and growl as countdown lights flash. At the green light the darts zing off down the track. Jack tracks them around the first turn and says "Funny, I thought they would be much faster."

Jax says "They used to be yes, but then no one could keep track of them, a race you cannot watch is a waste of time."

Jack follows the progress of the blue dart, he leads the race but is under tight pressure from a green one. As they begin the second lap they elegantly sweep through the first turn side by side. The red dart makes it's presence felt by elbowing a yellow dart into the side of the track, then off he zings chasing the leading two. The red dart closes in on the green, but red is known for this tactic and green is ready, he forces the red to the outside pinning him behind blue. Blue pulls away and takes the win, Jack jumps up "Yes! the dirty racer lost, I win!"

"Well done," says Jax "You have a natural eye for competition."

Sue loosens her grip on the railing as she starts to get a little more used to the height. She looks across to the trees and imagines what may live amongst the branches there.

Between the races a box hovers up to the viewing globes, like a bee visiting flowers. It buzzes towards their doors and they open to let it in. There is small pale blue vendor/pilot sitting behind some snacks in the box. Roomp buys a few snacks and four drinks, the hovering vendor drifts off and attends another globe. "Here," says Roomp as he hands Sue and Jack their drinks "If you don't like the flavour you can change it with the button on the side there." A couple of button presses later and they are both enjoying their refreshment.

A different set of race darts arrive on the circuit. The same colour codes remain, though two are now blue. With the flick of a switch one changes to orange. Sue picks the winner this time, two wins in a row for team Earth. It is hard to study form on a random set of racers in random colours, all down to luck. It is as if the house do not wish such form followers.

The sixth race is preparing, the darts sit with their cockpits open as the pilots chat, while mechanics tinker with their tiny rockets. The racers of the red and blue darts seem to be having a disagreement, only bitter words fly between them, as breaking up a fight would be humiliatingly easy for the mechanics. So they strut back to their respective darts and climb aboard. When the lights twinkle on the starting line and the darts zip away, inevitably the red and blue darts tangle soon enough. Blue clipping red's wing and sending the red racer flying up the side of the track. For a moment it looks like the dart will leave the track and plunge to the ground to who knows how far below, but the dart grazes off some sort of invisible shield, there to keep the racers within the circuit, no death races here. No winners are picked for the sixth round in the viewing pod, though an adjacent pod is full of celebration.

Now the seventh race prepares. Sue and Jack do not know how much the bet was, it was not even their money, but the buzz of the bet remains and closer attention is observed. A more jovial grid climbs aboard their racing darts, the canopies close and the tweeting sounds to announce the clearing of the track as the darts hum and whirr ready to race again. They launch off the grid and into the first turn.

A mean looking black dart leading the way from red. Yellow holds the rest back with weaving lethargy. By half way through the race, yellow has been passed by green but green is too far behind now to win, it is between black and red. Either Sue wins, or does not. In the final lap red has lulled the black dart into a false sense of security, so red makes his move, dummying left then sweeping right and passing to take the win. Sue gives a big smile and shouts "Yes! you little *****!" Surprising all. "What did I win?" She asks Jax, "The bets are always quite small, fifty credits," he says and adds "The drinks were half a credit each, not so bad."

"Then the next round is on me" Says Sue.

18

Time for a break from the racing and a break for comfort. Roomp presses a button on the control and the globe sweeps back down to the lower level. The door opens and Sue gets out of the bubble, onto terra firma, and off to the bathroom. The lower portion of the circuit is empty, as most are still up in the globes, Jack, Jax and Roomp wait in a nearby restaurant for Sue. Jax attempts to translate the menu for Jack, "No, I don't believe any of it tastes like chicken, but it is all very safe, it has to be, as there are so many variations of stomach attending." Jack scrolls through the pictures and gives in saying "You pick something for us Jax, I have no idea." Jax pushes the orders into the menu pad. Jack notices no card inserted to pay, and asks

"Does the menu automatically take from the card in your pocket?"

"Oh no, food of this kind is free, snacks and changeling drinks are a small price."

"Free with the entry?"

"Food is free everywhere, it makes starvation impossible, or at least less likely, no matter how poor, there is always food to eat, and always shelter."

The food arrives at the same time as Sue, she says to Jack "Use those loos over there, they are much better." So Jack trots across to them right away.

Sue says "I see you ordered without me?", Jax replies "You would have chosen what?" Looking over the plates she says "Maybe something less blue."

As they eat they watch two small squirrel like creatures playing in some bushes across from them, they chase each other through the branches, one of them comes out into the open, crosses the walkway to the eating area in serpentine bounds. Some people from a few tables away sprinkle a little of their food for it, which it eats gratefully, then scampers back to the cover of the bushes. It is mid afternoon already on this shorter Knool day, some of the patrons are heading back to their ships to beat the rush, there is a constant swinging of globes as they are emptied. Jax asks "So you two, did you enjoy the races?" Sue says "It was better than I thought it would be, but I think I'd like to see some of the nature here." Jack nods in agreement "Yes, it would be amazing to see the wildlife of Knool."

"Very well" said Jax "Tomorrow we will go to a place I know of. You can see some of what Knool has to offer the naturist." This makes Jack laugh. Which makes Jax confused.

Queuing up at the Ship park, Sue and Jack people watch as the party await their turn to collect the ship. The winners and the losers are easy to discern, the families, well, they are just tired.

There is a distant clanking and whirring as the ship is unloaded from the rack and makes its way towards them. Jack suddenly remembers, "The pilot!? Has he been in there all that time?"

Jax shrugs "Oh yes, he does not enjoy the races, so stayed and plugged into the machine, he enjoys that."

"Seems a shame to stay inside on a day like this."

"It is always a day like this."

The ramp lowers, welcoming them in, getting onboard they make themselves comfortable in the passenger compartment.

"You know," Sue says to Jax "When we were first abducted, and we WERE abducted, I was not happy at all, in fact I wanted to take the ship and fly it back home." Jax nods "Yes, I did hear about that." Sue adds "You are lucky you have been so nice to us, but yes it has been interesting. It is not as if we have responsibility for our children any longer, they are grown and have their own responsibilities. So though I am not staying longer than I must, it has been enjoyable, and I have learned a great deal."

Jax smiles an appreciative smile, as the ship warms up. It then glides up into the evening air. The wind is already starting to pick up and the clouds are beginning to build and move at higher speed. The sky is lit in bronze as the sun starts to dip. Nothing more to see, as the night creatures are not willing to put on a show this evening. They arrive back at the base and quickly get back inside before the real winds hit.

Back in their room Sue and Jack get a little time alone, while the chefs prepare the evening meal. Sue says to Jack "Do you think they have one of those machines here? I'd like to have a book to read." Jack gets up off the bed "I'll go ask Roomp, I think I saw him by the dining room window earlier."

Out in the hall he can really feel the place vibrating from the vicious winds of Knool, he finds Roomp in the dinning room adjusting controls on a small desk, a wart protruding out from the immaculate clean wall, Jack asks "Busy?.. We were wondering if you had one of those machines? Like on the ship." Roomp finishes adjusting some fine controls then the desk slides back invisibly into the wall. "I was attending to the wind control, the direction is not as predicted, it should be more comfortable now, and yes of course, you will find they are in the cabinet in your room, I shall go with you, to show you how they work."

In the room Roomp opens the cabinet and retrieves a small box, inside are two little horseshoe shaped trinkets. He says "Tuck it over your left ear and press this button, the rest is in the machine." Sue surprised says "Wow, technology moves on fast." She attaches it over her ear and says "So, should I close my eyes or leave them open?" Roomp replies "Either way you choose, it projects straight to your brain. But perhaps we look less odd dreaming with our eyes closed."

So Sue lies back on the bed for a while, she goes to the library, to find a good book. Jack just lies back and watches the clouds tumble past the skylight, it would be time to eat soon anyway.

Eventually they rise from their slumber and amble to the dining room. The sentries remained at the entrance, Jack wonders if they are guarding them from some unseen malice, or if he and Sue are the threat. Perhaps they just love the smell of the food in the room.

Sue asks Roomp "Why do you have guards at the entrance of this dining room? Are we threatening? Is there someone outside who does not want us here?" Roomp says "It is traditional to guard our place of eating. Sometimes tradition looks ridiculous to fresh eyes, but from inside, it is always there and unquestioned. And it's a job." The evening meal is laid out once more on crystal platters. Looking more appetising now that they know the flavours, now some of the oddness has faded. Jax and Roomp eat with their guests again. Thinking of cultural difference, Sue looks at the pronged sticks they eat with here and says to Jax "In our culture, we have a knife in the right hand, a fork in the left, unless we only have a fork, then you use the right." Jack adds "But in the east they use sticks, or when we have Chinese food.. On friday night.." Sue continues "And in polite society, you don't put your elbows on the table and you don't speak with your mouth full." Jax politely nods.

All tradition only makes sense when you are within the society. From outside it always looks near madness.

Sue and Jack retire to their sleeping quarters, while Jax and Roomp continue to sit and sip their drinks. Their own dialect is quite whistley and squeaky as they speak to each other. Jax says "These two are handling this change in circumstance very well, it is good to see some interest and joy in what we intend to share."

"Stroop had better luck this time yes, that last being just couldn't wait to have his memory wiped. Every new thing brought new terror, even after a month he could not look

Stroop in the eyes. I believe Stroop had to pause him for a large part of the journey."

"I wonder what he is doing now? I hope he is enjoying the comfort of the ordinary." They then leave the sentries to their work and head for their own slumber.

19

The next day dawns, and butter wouldn't melt. The air is still and the clouds light and wispy in a friendly sky. Two large birds are wrestling in the tree tops, causing the tree to swing to and fro. The cause of the argument watches on from an adjacent tree. Loud screeches echo across the platforms and feathers fly, till one of the birds has to admit defeat and leaps from a branch and glides off, down to lower boughs, to attend to his crooked feathers. The victor sits proudly by his mate and flares his crest. She then flies off to hunt, as he preens.

Down on the landing platform, Ilena engineers are checking over a ship, an old robust looking craft having the appearance of a ballerina panda. Near the building, along the walkway, Jax speaks of shields and of backup systems to the pilot, as if this were a machine of war. Jack and Sue emerge out onto the platform with Roomp, who tells them "You will be heading out soon to see some of Knool's nature, final preparations are being made." Sue looks at the ship and enquires "Not using that pretty ship of yesterday? This one looks very old."

Jack adds "It looks functional, like a helicopter gunship.. is this a military ship?"

Roomp a little put out "Oh no, crafts of war are forbidden, this is designed to survive nature."

Both Jack and Sue share a glance that says 'What the hell sort of nature is out there'.

Jax greets them at the landing platform,

"All ready! Ready to go? We will hopefully see many exciting sights today."

Sue asks "Do you not have zoos to see animals?"

"Zoos?"

"Yes, zoos. A place to keep animals in cages to see them safely, keeps them safe too."

"Lock up nature? To keep them safe from what?"

"To keep them safe from people shooting them."

"So you lock nature in, so your own people do not shoot them? How odd, I would suggest not shooting them would be easier for all."

"Yes, but it is complicated.."

Jack avoids the conversation and heads to the pilot. "Preep? Is that you?"

"Yes, is that you Jack?"

Jack laughs, but is unsure if Preep was joking "Yes, of course it's me, you are taking me and Sue to the wilds of Knool? Very exciting."

"We are leaving right away, so if you could please enter."

Jax, Sue and Jack climb the steps into the dark cramped compartment. Preep climbs into the pilot seat, some lighting flickers into life in the passenger compartment, it is rather dusty and looks well used, the bench seats are sagging, and there is a musty smell, as if this were well used fifty years ago, it reminds them both of the saucer. Jack asks Jax "Is Roomp not joining us today?"

"Sorry no, he does not like this sort of thing, nature can be quite rough."

The craft hums into life and Preep's trademark smooth piloting skills show as the trees sweep past the window before they are even aware they have left the platform. Jax reassures Sue and Jack "Do not worry, the shielding on this ship is very good, both engines are newly serviced."

Jack presses his nose to the small window and watches the tall trees flash past in a blue green blur under the aqua sky, a sight that is always extraordinary to visiting eyes. Patches of orange grassland appear and a glimpse of what looks like a herd of dinosaurs in multicoloured geometric patterned coats.

A lake appears in the window, glistening jewels dance across the surface in the bright sunshine, dark foreboding shadows lurk beneath, chasing shoals of alien string eels.

The water gives way to patchy woodlands of twisted blue leafed trees. The craft then slows so Preep can pick out a place to land. He finds a well trodden clearing and the ship descends.

The dust billows around the ship as it settles onto its landing stalks. Jax tells Jack and Sue of his plan, "First we will just sit and wait, as our landing may have scared the cowsaurs off, but I am sure they will be back to that small spring soon, and they bring the attention of the predators, most likely velocsabres or maybe a rare boshark, the ship will have its shield on maximum projection, but this still only gives a short safe zone around the ship, so please stay close. Here are some binoglasses to wear." They fiddle with the arm adjustments to fit them properly, then experiment with the zoom. Jack says, "Whoah don't try to walk with them on full zoom, that's a crazy trip."

They all put their nose to the windows looking for signs of animals. After a while some large hairy dinosaur like creatures come to the spring and take a drink. These look like the same species Jack spotted earlier while in the air, their long necks reach down to the water, while others keep watch for danger. Jax presses the door release and they edge out into the fresh air.

All is quiet except for the hum of the ship, powered up still to run the shield. They put on their glasses and get a closer look at the creatures by the water. Sue says "They must be about twenty feet high, only seen anything like these in a museum, just bones, and not hairy and certainly not so colourful. They look like hippie dinosaurs," Jack laughs, "Yeah hippie dinosaurs, exactly."

Another group of smaller two legged creatures now arrive, pale blue skin, same as the leaves of the gnarled trees scattered around the clearing, short necks and stubby tailed, they have to squat down to drink next to their neighbours.

All three observers drift away from the ship a little to get a feeling of the wild openness of the outdoors in this peaceful scene. Jax hears a noise behind him, Preep is tapping the cockpit window to get their attention. He beckons them to come closer to the ship. Jax waves a don't worry hand, but Preep is insistent so they come closer to the ship, Preep gets Jax attention again and points to the undergrowth to the right. Jax adjusts his glasses and peers in the general direction Preep is pointing, then he spots a head amongst the foliage, a head of darkest blue with long teeth criss crossing in its jaws and large amber eyes staring intently across at the watering hole. Jax tugs at Jacks tunic to gain attention and gives the universal shush sign and they quietly back towards the ship.

Over at the watering hole the animals are still unaware, no hand claps to startle, no warnings, they watch nature play out. One of the cowsaurs moves to the right of the watering hole, ever nearer the waiting blue boshark, the cowsaur turns and arches it's long neck down to the water, then zing! in an explosion of energy the beast uncoils from its hiding place in a flurry of leaves, launching itself at the huge animals neck, great long coils of body wrap around the poor cowsaur and rows of claws tear into its flesh, they both spiral into the air as the animal tries to buck the thing off of its neck, it tries to run, but the tail of the predator takes its legs from under it and it lands in a heap, shaking the ground beneath the feet of the stunned onlookers. The boshark tightens its coils around the neck and soon the struggle ends.

The rest of the animals are nowhere to be seen now. They retreated back into the trees, while the three visitors were transfixed by the brutality of nature. In a few minutes it is noticed the kill has attracted the attention of flying scavengers, a flock of dark birds fly in tight clouds high above the prone cowsaur, so the boshark greedily tears into the flesh, eating quickly before the birds descend to eat.

Sue and Jack catch their breath, it is not something they have ever seen the like of before, nor ever likely to see again. They share looks of amazement with Jax and watch as the boshark gulps down its last mouthful, then it slinks off back into the scrub. "Time to get back inside" says Jax, so they climb into the craft and close the door, continuing to watch the action through the window, the invisible shield being a net, not designed to shield from a tiny threat such as these birds. The cloud of birds descend quickly, engulfing the animal. The corpse seems to be vibrating from the constant energy of the birds feeding. In the screeching intensity of these flying piranha, soon only bones remain and the birds rise back up as one. Then nothing, no creature, no sound, just the humming of the ship. Jax breaks the silence, "Would you like to see some gentler nature? There are some creatures near the coast, a most beautiful display." Sue says "Please, something nice and calming."

"Of course," says Jack. Preep gets the OK signal, and the ship lifts off. Leaving what is left of the creature to its resting place alone.

20

For a change of view Preep steers the ship way up high, swiftly the craft is amongst the wispy clouds. From here they see the arch of the horizon and below them the trees stretch for mile after mile, and in the distance dark mountains climb into the sky. Though Preep instead swings the craft out towards the sea.

Diving now, the ship shears at the air towards the ground, then the sea. Preep allows himself some flair in his flying once more, pulling up at the last second barely skimming across the water, he pulls at the controls swinging back around to dry land. Jack is really enjoying the acrobatics as he watches the wake of spray out of the window.

Sue is not enjoying it quite so much, grabbing the hand holds tightly, "What happened to the smooth magic carpet ride?" Jack smiles "Got to have a little fun in life."

So as not to disturb the creatures they came to see, Preep gets back to his smooth piloting, while he looks for a suitable spot to set down. He finds a small piece of grassland behind the coasts uninviting jet black jagged rocks and gently sets down.

The engine sinks to a low hum again and Jax says "Anyone hungry?" and pulls a box from under his seat. Sue's stomach isn't just rumbling from the extravagant flight, "Oh yes, seems hours since we last ate anything." Jax opens the box, hands out some snacks in packs and drink bottles. Taking one bar, he hands it to Jack saying "Try this one, it is quite delicious." Jack tears open the wrapper and takes a bite, and pulls a face like he just chomped into the sourest lemon, "Hell Jax, that's sharp!" then says "Here Sue, try this, it'll turn your face inside out."

"You make it sound so tempting…" She then takes a small bite anyway, "Woah! Jax, if you wanted to kill us, this is a really elaborate way of going about it."

Jax apologetic "Sorry, try this one instead."

These snacks go down much better, and they sip the familiar changeling drinks. After they finish Jax packs the box back under his seat then says "Right, the shield is on again, but we don't expect any trouble here, but just in case, do not go too far beyond the rocks." Sue and Jack nod and follow Jax out of the door.

Staying quiet they approach the rocks. Leaning on a large boulder, they peer across to a small light blue sandy beach in a bay. Jack whispers to Jax, "What are we looking at? Nothing here but all these little bushes." Jax says "They are a little later than usual, or we are early .. Soon."

They sit and watch the bushes, and then they watch the surf lap against the sand. They watch the orange grass sway in the breeze and listen to nothing but the waves.

Then one bush moves and pops up on two tall twig legs, blue leaves form into wings that stretch and flap, a fluffy crested head with a long hooked beak unravels from within the bush. The creature lets out a shrill squack. Bushes start popping up all amongst the foliage, all stretching and preparing, ten then twenty, shortly hundreds of these masters of disguise are flapping and squacking all over the beach. Jax says "Wait."

At one end of the flock one of the creatures suddenly flashes yellow, this causes the next to react, then the next, a yellow wave washes across the flock, then red, then to green. One takes to the air clumsily, looking for all this world like a rotund rider trying to mount a horse for the first time. As with any flock, it is the sign for all to follow. The rainbow flock heaves into the air. Their wings squeaking as a wood pigeon's. They all head off, out to sea in a wonderful watercolour swirl, to go fish.

As the multi coloured flock leaves, in an adjacent bay they notice some more goings on. A large fish is crawling up the beach, four elongated fins carry it across the sand. It pauses and seems to hold an ear to the ground, if it had ears. One pause more then the fish dives into the sand. The sand flies, the tail flaps, as it wrestles whatever is below. In a struggle it returns to the surface and gobbles up the sand grub before turning back to the sea, to wash dry land's filth from its scales.

Towards the mountains it is noted that the sky is darkening and swirling, looking like a goth lava lamp. Jax says "Time to get back to base, the rain is coming tonight, and perhaps it will beat the sunset." Back aboard the ship, Preep is already warming the it up, he has seen the latest weather report. As soon as his passengers are settled into their seats, Preep heaves the ship into the air and begins the race with the weather back to base.

21

Back on Earth. John is in the garden on a November evening, the air is crisp in smell, sound and temperature, as only this time of year can be. Though November has brought a stiff chill, he is determined to use the rear deck. It has been a tough year so far and good news is to be celebrated, a celebration for Jenny and Pamela's engagement. He turns on the outdoor heaters and adjusts the controls, turning them up full. He sorts through some CDs and slips a Tom Waits album into his old stereo. He listens to the opening track as he lays the table, fiddles with some lights, "Yes Tom, somewhere.." he says to himself.

Inside, Julie is putting food on the plates, dealing out fish and vegetables. Jenny is pouring the wine and Pamela is drinking it. Jenny tempts fate saying "It's still not raining, I think it is going to stay dry."

"Don't say that," says Pamela "You'll make it rain."

Jenny fusses over portions, "Is that enough veg for you Pam?"

"Yes, stop worrying, it's fine, lets go eat."

They take their seats and toast to the engagement. John toasts "To Jen and Pam, may all your days together be as beautiful as you two." They eat and chat of television, of brainless politicians and a lack of a decent summer before we got sunk into the winter again.

Julie plays restlessly with her food then says "Actually we have some news too, I'm pregnant!"

Jenny gives a polite, 'This is our night, but congratulations' smile and says "Oh how lovely, congratulations, how far along are you?"

"Seven weeks, so far, so good, touch wood."

Another toast, "To the future," says Pamela.

"Mum and Dad would have been really happy to see you two get hitched," said John.

Jenny takes a sip of wine then adds "You never know, I think they're still out there.. Anyway, to Mum and Dad."

Many toasts and many bottles into the late evening. Well, just one more glass for Julie.

Preep is pointing the ship directly at the tumultuous sky. They and the weather heading for the same place. A fair race with how the wind howls on this planet. Then the lightning starts, just ahead of the thunderous explosions as sound catches up with light. Jax announces "It's going to be closer than we predicted, hang on tight and strap yourself down to the seat." Preep accelerates into the edge of the storm and the ship starts to vibrate, the incoming clouds have brought premature darkness, only broken by the blinding flash of the lightning bolts, illuminating furrowed brows. Jax looks a little more tense than before, heavy weather, even for a Knool night. They feel the ship slow and swing around to approach the platform, Preep wrestles with the controls in the increasing wind. A settling force is felt as they are near touch down. Roomp has engaged the landing beam from inside the base.

Even when on the platform and clamped down, the wind rattles the little ship about like a leaf on a branch. Sue asks "So, how do we get from here to the base?" Jax replies "A good question." As the rain starts to batter the windows of the ship. "Do not worry, we shall go the back way." A faint rumbling is heard and stomachs leap, as the ship drops below the surface of the deck. They leave the weather above them, while they sink into the comfort of the base. The air outside the ship settles, as doors are sealed.

They exit their brave little ship, relieved. Jax pats his pockets and says "Lets go get something to eat."

So they leave the mechanics to scamper around the ship and check it is secure, while the three adventurers walk through the hidden lower corridors. These are very much more for function rather than beauty. Like the corridors of the saucer, a little dusty and worn. Sue asks "Do you ever clean down here?" Jax replies with no whiff of impatience "Oh yes we have automated cleaning, though the corners are somewhat neglected." The whole place vibrates with the wind outside and despite the distance they can still hear the rain lashing at the outer walls. The lights flicker as another gust hits, they press the button for the lift to go up, out of the shade, back into the plush place above.

22

The group meet Roomp in the hall, Jax asks him "Have you adjusted the wind sails?", Roomp says "Yes they are set, though at their limit. I'm going to go make sure the cakes are ok."

In the dining room the food has still reached the table and the sentries still stand, if a little wobbly from time to time in the stronger gusts, amongst all the double checking that things are tied down, dinner continues.

Jack, Sue, Roomp and Jax settle to eat at the table. The lights still occasionally flicker but not so often, the group are starting to feel like the station will hold together and survive another battering from this monstrous weather. Sue asks "So Jax, it has been great, but are you ready to ask us the questions now, so we can head back tomorrow?"

"It's more of a feeling really than an asking of questions. I feel good about what I have learned and shall report back my findings to those on Ool."

Jack quite stunned "So thats it? We are heading back? I thought I might go fishing.."

Sue interjects "I'm sure there is no fishing here, even if there were, who know who would win between you and a fish."

"Hey!.. Really Jax, thank you, it has been amazing, we've seen such wonderful things, things we will never forget."

Jax mops his chin and replies "I am glad you enjoyed it, we do love to share new experiences with our guests."

Jax goes out of the room returning with a large bottle of drink, and says "To celebrate new adventures." Then pours a healthy glass for all. Sue takes a long swig and says "This stuff is growing on me."

"One thing that has occurred to me Jax," said Jack, "With these nights, do you ever see the stars?"

Jax takes a swig then replies "Oh yes, on rare occasion we do see the stars, on especially calm nights. Perhaps this is why we tried so hard to reach them, they were hanging there only long enough for us to wish to see them more often."

Sue thinks and says "But you're originally from Ool? You got here from there?" Jax says "Haha well remembered, but the Ilena are from Ool, they brought the technology to us, well, added to our plans. I am Streen, of Knool".

The storm still rages outside and vibrant clouds race across the sky, sending forth coloured lightning, lighting the interior of the base in rainbow flashes. Jack and Sue go to the hallway to watch the storm rage, leaving Jax and Roomp at the table.

The two friends continue to drink and talk, Jax says "Tomorrow we will take them to breakfast at Shewna, then the goodbyes."

"Then return them to their home, all this forgotten."

"Yes, sadly, all forgotten."

It is getting into the night proper now, but the rain is abating and the lightning is heading out to sea to shock the fish. Jack keeps watching and soaking it in, while Sue heads for a wee, wash and to turn in. Jack thinks of all the animals out there, way down on the ground sheltering from such terrible conditions every night. Surely there must be some crazy nocturnal ones too, trying to make their living in this, sleeping through the glorious day. But maybe not, surely a foolish way to live. He finally heads to bed and finds Sue already asleep. He goes to snuggle up, but the join where they shoved the beds together is right where he wants to be, so he rolls back and gazes out of the skylight as the clouds waltz once again, before drifting off to sleep.

23

The morning bursts out with renewed enthusiasm, burning away the night's rain, a watercolour haze hovers over the trees as the morning dew turns to vapour. Jack, Sue and Roomp stand under the hallway arches, watching the world wake up. In the distance Roomp spots a tree split in two by last nights lightning. Jack asks Roomp "How often do you get a storm like that?"

"Rarely enough to be surprised, often enough to be ready."

Jax arrives around the corner and spies the nature watchers in the hall, "Ready for breakfast? The ship is prepared."

Sue says "Oh yes, always room for a second breakfast." Jack looks at his shoes, and fesses up "We may have got a little bit too peckish."

Jax says "Do not worry, a comfortable appearance is healthy."

They head to the platform and a familiar sleek ship is waiting for them, looking beautiful, glistening with the morning dew. Sue says "I'll miss this limousine service back on earth."

Settling into the seats they look at the holographic menu on the table. Roomp points out "You had this kind of food last time, you said that you liked it," Sue says "It doesn't look like something I'd like."

Jax replies "It doesn't look as good in the pictures."

The ship eases into the air and spears off across the treetops heading inland. Jack and Sue look to the windows and spot a few familiar animals starting their new day with an argument.

In a short time they start to see some buildings in among the trees, they reside amongst the upper branches in groups of luminous discs. The ship slows and they hover a moment before heading straight down between a copse of trees.

Endless tree trunks rise up past the windows and the light starts to fade beneath the vast canopy, down, down and down. The forest floor is covered in debris of fallen leaves, twigs and curly curiously coloured mushrooms sprouting around the tree trunks. The ship lands gracefully on the roof of the restaurant. The four of them walk out into the pungent forest air, towards the lift to take them down into the building.

The restaurant is a large pristine white bagel shaped building. Windows sweep all the way around its circumference, in the centre is the kitchen. It is early, so as they are the first customers, they have the pick of the seating. Sue takes the lead and gets a seat by the window, looking in towards the centre, to watch the goings on with arrivals and service coming and going. Jack takes a seat next to Sue, Jax and Roomp sit opposite.

They take another attempt at the menu while they wait for the waiter. It takes a little while for news to travel that there are customers already. Roomp picks his favourite and Jax suggests "Try the loorn … It's very good," he adds. Sue in 'devil may care' mood says "OK, what's to lose, what are you having Jack?" Jack studies the menu, changing his mind several times, as the waiter arrives. A tall fellow, even thinner than the Ilena, barely any room for frame beneath his translucent skin, piercing green eyes gaze around the group "klinm ssllkk weel?" he asks, Jax says "Oh yes, I'll have to translate, Liif ennn suulo." and points to the menu. Orders taken, the waiter wafts away. Sue asks Roomp "Which door is the bathroom?"

He points saying "The one over there, with picture on it." Sue squints and sees the graphic picture, "Well, that is to the point.. back in a minute."

Up above, there are faint rumblings as two more ships arrive, the group wait and watch, they see the lift lights change. An Ilena and a smaller furry friend exit the lift. They head out of sight for a seat on the other side of the restaurant. By the time the second party arrive, a seating attendant has decided to attend, perfect timing for him. The four rather large customers do not look very happy and seem to be embarking on an animated discussion with the newly set upon attendant. After a few more exchanges the attendant disappears off behind staff doors. The disgruntled group stare expectantly at the door, as it opens. The waiter comes out of the door showing off his long dextrous hands, holding all four plates. He takes a sideways glance at the staring customers as he heads to the table.

Jax guides the plates under the correct noses. As the waiter disappears to get the drinks. There is a sensation of movement and stomachs momentarily drop, Sue says "What was that, an earthquake?"

Roomp replies "The argument earlier, our unhappy friends over there, they have come a long way and want a view."

Sue looks over her shoulder and sees the ground slowly dropping away. The slightly happier group across from them go take a seat.

They watch through the window as the trees pass downwards. The endless trunks, then the branches, till finally they clear the canopy and the mountains come into view, the plains lie in the mountain's shadow, in pink mist far away beyond the forest.

Finally the restaurant settles, two hundred feet above the five hundred foot high trees. Making it feel rather precarious to Sue. She feels for sway or feeling of unease, but no further movement is felt at all. Jax sees that Sue looks uneasy and says, "Do not worry, the projectors hold the building even more precisely than if it were on the ground." It seems to be true, so they enjoy the view and start to pick at their meals.

Sue's blue cabbage type thing tastes kind of meaty and the yellow sauce kind of fruity, but things are starting to tumble into some sort of new sense. Jax asks "Have you thought about staying? You could stay."

Roomp interjects "No you cannot stay."

"It is an interesting thought," Jack says,

Sue adds "You couldn't put us up forever for free."

"Well, we could do that yes, but humans do not have a permanent pass yet, that is the blockage," said Roomp,

"And we are expected back," said Sue.

Another ship is heard to arrive, a distant thrump on the roof way above, an elegant couple, seven feet tall and having multiple limbs enter. The most alien of races Sue and Jack have encountered so far. All shapes and sizes seen, but all the previous having two of each limb, the new arrivals notice the humans intently watching them and shyly disappear around the other side of the restaurant.

Through the glass they see a ship approaching, it bobs up and down, and weaves from side to side, then hovers outside the window, it circles around the restaurant while looking in. Half way around it gets to where the group are sat and comes in a little closer. Two figures are leaning forward in the cockpit, the shorter one leans forwards, waves and smiles. Jax returns the wave and beckons them to come on in. The pilot sits back and the little ship rises out of view.

"These are your companions for the return Journey," said Roomp,

"A characterful pair," said Jack.

24

The restaurant's lift door opens and the pilots walk in. Both of Ilena race, one tall and officious looking, with electronic clipboard in hand and the other shorter, more portly and enthusiastic. Roomp stands "May I introduce Jeak your pilot and Woodel your captain for the journey back."

"Pleased to meet you," said Jack and offers a hand to hover empty in the air. Jeak grabs a pair of seats from another table and drags them to their table, making a tooth rattling screech across the floor. "Are you ordering?" said Jax. Jeak pats his stomach and says "No no, we ate before we came." Then he settles down and starts to pick at the food on Roomp's plate while he catches up with the latest news with Jax.

Sue looks over the shoulder of Woodel, watching him make adjustment on his clipboard, small graphs dance and writing blips across the page, Woodel notices this and turns it away. "OK time to settle up and head back," says Jax and he presses a button on the table, three meals flash up on the screen and prices in alien language. Sue notes this and asks "Just three meals?"

"Yes," said Jax "Roomp always eats from the free menu."

They stack the plates ready for the waiter to pick up, then head for the lift.

Up on top of the restaurant the ship park is getting busy, overdue some of the folks finishing up and leaving.

Jack looks over Jeak's little craft, it's tiny wings and comic bulbous cabin, "Don't worry, we are not taking you back in this," said Jeak. He and Woodel board and take off in haphazard flight back to the base. The rest following in their more graceful transport, in more graceful flight. They take the long way home, to watch the leap of the shein at the shore and the running grent on the orange plane.

As the base comes into view they see a ship waiting on the landing pad. Technicians fuss around it, preparing it for flight. It rests bulbous yet elegant, like a great white shark. The pristine bodywork glistening in the sun. Jeak's tiny craft sits next to it, a comical tiny bug beside the cruise ship.

As they get nearer and land beside it, Sue and Jack get a better feel for the size of this ship, they get a feeling of how ridiculous the size this ship is. It would be a nonsense to carry just four souls in such a vessel. They disembark down the walkway of their swish little day trip ship, Jeak comes to greet them "Quite a beauty isn't she? and fast too, you will be back on earth in less than a week."

Jack nods, he turns around to take in the surroundings, with some sadness. Hoping that if he concentrates the memories will fix more firmly. Sue leans on the platform's railing and fiddles with the cuticles on her fingers, she glances left and sees a familiar sight. Betsy is sat on the back of some sort of transporter hovering along the walkway.

Jax approaches Jack "We removed your transport, the engineers had an interesting time learning of it's technology."

"Oh excellent," said Jack "I thought I was going to have to walk home. Not from here, when we are, there.. on earth, you know what I mean.."

Jack bites his nails as he watches Betsy waver up into the hold on a light beam projected from the transporter, wheels dangling and sump dripping, on her way in undignified carriage. Happy that his noble steed is safely aboard, Jack and Sue wander along the walkway and look out into the trees for last sightings of exotic creatures. They take some moments to take in the calm warm turquoise sky of a Knool midday. Across under the ship, engineers are unplugging umbilical cords and dispersing. Leaving the great white shark independent.

Jeak and Woodel approach, Jeak tells them "It is time to go, are you ready?" Woodel stands sternly beside him, with his ever present clipboard, looking Jack and Sue over, updating his information. "Yes," said Sue, "Ready as we'll ever be."

They followed them back towards the ship, where Roomp and Jax wait. Jax gives both of them unexpected warm hugs, "Wonderful to meet you two, I hope you enjoyed it, who knows, the council may grant the pass this time and you may come again." Roomp offers his hand to Jack, which Jack takes and enthusiastically shakes, "Good luck and enjoy the memories," Roomp says.

Woodel interjects to say "If you would please follow me."

The ship appears sleek but for the landing gear and a small lift protruding down from it's chin. A glass elevator in a glass tube. The door opens and all four of them get in.

They rise up into the ship and the lift door opens. Inside the ship is pristine, a natural light emits from the ceiling, illuminating untouched white floors and crisp white walls, any brighter and they would need sunglasses.

25

Entering through a lethally fast sliding door, they come to a lounge area, as an airport lounge would be, given a blank cheque. Plush seats and deep pile carpet, various gadgets flicker and flash on coffee tables. Both Sue and Jack kick off their shoes and walk onto the carpet, wiggling their toes to feel the plushness beneath their feet. Jeak points out the electronic menu on the coffee table and where the virtual reality machines reside in cubby holes in the arms of the chairs and also where the toilet is. Once they feel their guests have settled in he and Woodel leave them to it and go prepare for launch.

Sue takes a seat and gets the virtual reality ear piece out to look at, checking it is the same as those at the base. Jack sits in the seat, closes his eyes and curls his toes in the deep pile carpet. A humming is heard in the distance and soon after, movement. They both realise at once there is no window to catch a glimpse of the planet as they leave. On one side the wall is curved, with a simple switch adjacent, Jack takes a chance and presses the switch.

The risk rewarded, a panel sweeps away into the ceiling revealing a large window. They both lean on the sill and watch those magnificent trees sweep past, the shore arrives, the twinkling sea passes below them at accelerated rate before the ship pulls up.

The light pristine blue sky soon darkens, till it turns to the blackness of space. Leaning around with faces pressed to the glass, Knool shrinks, then finally disappears.

Jack presses the switch again to close the window just in case, remembering Stroop's warning. The ship settles to a quiet hum and no shake or tilt is felt. Sue goes to the bathroom and as Jack sits back down, he thinks of what they have experienced, and imagines how to convey the unimaginable to those who have not seen it.

Jeak comes in and says "Well how was that? Not as good as Preep, but not bad."

Jack gives a smile "Not bad at all, we watched from the window there, I hope you don't mind, I guessed the right switch."

Jeak waves it off "No problem, there is no eject button in here, you only risk accidentally ordering food on the electable."

Jeak attempts to explain a table top game to Jack, like animated chess, but the rules seem hard to grasp. Jeak gives in and exits to attend to the ship once again, leaving Jack and Sue to fiddle with buttons and relax.

They sit and spend time on nothing in particular for a while, but after a time Jack starts to take a queazy turn. Sue looks concerned, holding his pallid face she says "You don't look too well Jack, you have gone very pale, are you feeling ok?"

Jack holds his stomach and groans "No, not well at all, I think I ate something bad."

"The bathroom is right there if you need it, I'm going to go find Jeak."

As she searches the corridors, Sue's memory thinks of stomach pains in alien lands, and for the first time since the first few days Sue's emotions rise, not in anger this time, but in panic, Sue shouts "Jeak!? Preep? Woody? where are you?"

She finds Woodel with clipboard in hand. She grasps his arm saying "Come quick, Jack is going to give birth!"

Sue leads a slightly befuddled Woodel back to the lounge area, to where Jack is absent. They soon hear him performing a jazz solo in the bathroom. Sue bangs on the door and shouts through it "Are you ok Jack? Hold on, I've got Woodel."

The music abates and a very pale Jack emerges bent double shuffling out of the bathroom. Woodel looks Jack up and down and makes a note. Woodel likes a tight ship, and this is quite the opposite. He says "Would you follow me please". Sue holds the now frail Jack around the waist as they forlornly walk around the corridors following Woodel to the medical bay.

The door swishes open and inside are two metal beds, high up on pillars. Overhead lamps bring light to every crevice. Woodel asks "If you would get undressed please." Jack removes his clothes gingerly. Coyly stopping at his underpants, Sue then helps him up onto the bed. She watches as Woodel presses a button on the wall, releasing a tray from within. Various gadgets are laid out on the tray, probes and prongs and a gun of some sort, Woodel takes the gun.

Sue is naturally worried at such an array and says "Is he going to be OK? Be careful." There is no choice but trust.

26

Woodel twists a dial on the gun and through its fan shaped muzzle a light beam appears in red, he twists the dial again and the light changes through green to blue. He looks to Sue and says "Jack is going to be well." Then he points the fanned beam at Jack's head.

The beam cast no shadow, in fact it passes straight through his flesh as Woodel moves the beam slowly down his body. Traces of red appear in the beam all the way down his throat and more in his stomach then the lower intestine, and below. As the light passes his hands, there, spotted by expert eye his finger nails light ever so slightly red. Woodel says "There, the problem."

Sue turns to her husband "How many times have I told you not to bite your nails?"

A cabinet emerges from the wall, Woodel looks through various bottles and returns to Jack, "Take two of these, you will be well soon, then eat something. After washing your hands."

In the dining hall the sound echoes as they walk in this expansive hall. It is clearly made for many more guests. Sue and Jack sit at one of the tables. They flick through the menu and see a couple of things they have eaten before and enjoyed. Sue looks across and notices Jack's cheeks are returning to their normal rosy colour, "You are looking better," she says.

Jack rubs his stomach "Yes I feel much better, but I'm very hungry, I feel as empty as a politician's promise!"

Jeak comes into the dining hall from the kitchen carrying a couple of changeling drinks and takes a seat, "There you are, have you chosen? Just press here and it sends it through to the kitchen." He points, then takes a sip of Jack's drink. Jack moves his drink out of Jeak's reach, and presses the button to change the flavour a couple of times, "This ship, isn't it overkill? I mean, it's massive for just taking two of us back home."

Jeak eyes the drinking cup, then says "Well, we were expecting your planet to have been accepted by now, to be sharing more, but there have been, issues."

Sue says "Issues? how do you mean?"

Jeak rubs his neck and replies "Your planet was making progress for many years, but now seems to be slowing. The committee seem unsure as to why this would be. Other planets that were once behind, are now ahead, perhaps your planet is a little.. backward."

Jack looks at Sue to gauge how this is taken, but to his surprise Sue says "Sounds about right."

There is a ping from the direction of the kitchen, "Dinner's ready," announces Jeak and leaves to go retrieve it. Sue asks Jack "So, what is the story when we return, were we kidnapped by terrorists for ransom?"

"I don't know, I haven't thought about it, just gone day to day."

"This whole alien thing will have to go, they'd lock us away."

If Jack was a cartoon, a light bulb would appear and light over his head "Does your phone have a camera?"

"I think so. Maybe, but that went with all the bits and pieces in the car."

"Maybe they put it all back in, I wonder if we can find Betsy."

Self conscious silence falls as Jeak comes back with dinner.

Jeak places a plate in front of Sue "There you are, yours was the eeeeemp wasn't it Sue?"

"Maybe," said Sue. Both enjoy the meal as their minds twinkle with mild mischievousness giving them energy, and Jack is also brimming with oomph due to the medication.

After a brief game of 'keep the food out of Jeak's reach', they leave the one man flight crew to clear up. They head in the general direction of where they think Betsy might be, then wander back and forth through the long corridors. But nothing hangar like is found. Clearly they are going to have to try to use a lift. Sue presses what looks like the lift button and lights blink hopefully over the door. When the door opens they find Woodel occupying the lift. He says "Were you going to retrieve this?" and holds up the phone in his hand, Jack, flustered says "Oh no, just going to go check on the old girl make sure she is OK."

"Yes, thank you, how kind of you to bring it to us," said Sue.

Woodel ticks off something on his clipboard then says "Sorry but I cannot allow communications at this point."

Jack interrupts "Not for phoning, we just wanted to take a picture or two."

Woodel makes another mark on his ever present clipboard "No evidence can be taken, sorry."

Woodel shows Jack how to use the lift, then keeps a close eye as the door closes and watches as they descend to the lower deck. Jack opens the door and they leave the lift, the air is out of their balloon. If they could find a fire extinguisher they would let it off, to unreel the mischief that sits. They explore anyway, poking their heads in various closets and rooms of unknown use. They find a room with an entirely padded interior and Sue says "This is either for really horrible times, or really fun times." Jack pokes his head around the door "Looks like fun times, with all these cushions and pillows."

They find Betsy at last and look through their belongings in the back with a faint flutter of finding the phone, despite knowing exactly where it is, the mind is funny like that. Jack eyes some writing on a magazine and notes "It seems pretty dark down here now, lets go back up and have a drink."

"No argument here, I need a drink."

As they exit the lift it is darker on the upper deck also. They wonder if perhaps they are just tired. Jeak approaches along the corridor so Jack asks "Is it my tired eyes, or is it getting darker in here?"

Jeak replies "Oh yes, the lighting has a routine, to simulate night and day, to keep the body's clock on time, much less confusing than those old ships."

"Stroop just said he slept when tired."

"Oh he is such a funny one. Come, time for a drink."

They adjourn to a smaller lounge opposite the dining hall, a place to unwind it seems, a bar of sorts with small intimate tables. Jeak meanders over to the bar, returning with three metal tumblers and a bottle.

He splashes three measures into the tumblers and sets the bottle down. Jack takes his and holds it aloft "Cheers, to home." With no explanation or translation needed, Jeak taps the tumbler to Jack and Sue's "To home." Sue takes a swig then takes a breath, the drink is smooth yet potent, Sue asks Jeak "Do you have any kids Jeak?"

"Reproduction is the aspiration of a disease..? Then he checks himself "No offence meant. And you?"

Sue eyes Jeak carefully and takes another sip, "Three," she says "We miss them." Jack raises the mood and raises his drink "To adventure."

Sue clinks Jack's tumbler "Adventure." Sinks the drink, then takes the bottle to top up the tumblers.

27

John is wresting the Christmas tree into the stand, while Julie untangles the lights. Baby Jack is investigating the glass baubles, looking at his strange warped reflection in the blue and red globes, he picks one up and goes to bite it. Julie takes them and puts them out of harms way. Stick to the plastic ones this year.

John stands back admiring his handiwork and checks the tree is straight, "Not bad, not brushing the ceiling this year."

"Smaller tree, smaller family," says Julie mournfully, and yanks at the tangled wires. "How do they always get so tangled?" John goes over and takes an end and starts to help unthreading them, "At least we don't have to go through and check every bulb anymore."

Jack goes through the decorations, tugging on tinsel, waving plastic candy canes, chewing rocking horses and looking up the fairies dress, starting early.

In half an hour the tree is dressed, but till nearer the day, still bare about it's feet. John tries the lights, they begin to twinkle through their coloured routine. Then the cards go on the mantlepiece, red sashes sweep across the fire place, ribbons adorn the lamps and a sparkling nativity scene resides beside the phone. All the things to bring Christmas to a home.

The next morning, or simulated morning, as electric light breaks. Sue and Jack wake up in their bed, in their room, no clouds floating overhead, no view of the sky, just a crisp white ceiling so featureless to give snow blindness.

Jack swings his legs out of the bed and shuffles off to the bathroom as Sue lays and groans of light and of too much. On the way back to bed Jack's bleary eyes spot Woodel stiff and upright as ever, Woodel looks Jack up and down, then makes a mark on his clipboard and walks on. Jack feels lucky it was not a cold morning.

When he gets back to the room Sue is fiddling with the VR ear piece, Jack asks "You going to the library already? I'm going to get dressed and get some breakfast."

"Just quickly, I'll be there soon."

In the dining hall, Jeak is already there staring into a bowl of something hot and steaming while holding his head.

"No cure for a hangover yet?" joked Jack.

Jeak rubs his neck and straightens, "Oh yes, just waiting a short while for it to work."

"Do you have some for us too?"

He stirs the bowl and says "The medicine is in the breakfast, I'm on my third bowl."

He orders two more bowls on the menu, before continuing his journey to the bottom of his present bowl. In a few minutes a ping from the kitchen. Jeak goes and gets the bowls and sets them on the table "Is Sue coming for breakfast?"

"Yes soon. Well, who knows." Jack tastes the porridge and winces a little, "So Jeak, how does these ships fly so fast without hitting anything?"

"Apart from other ships, there is nothing else to hit. The planets are designed to collect stray pieces to keep the lanes clear. My theory is that planets just hold us to the surface as a side effect."

"So meteors are just the collection of space junk? How about comets? They just keep going."

"Comets are a glitch, no one's perfect, we have them tracked and know where not to be."

"So, the whole universe was built to self tidy and life was a side effect?"

Jack laughs, stirs his breakfast, then goes to see where Sue got to.

Sue is sat up in bed, earpiece in and catching flies. Jack gently shakes her shoulder, "Wake up sleepy head, breakfast is getting cold."

"I'll be there soon, don't fuss."

"I have never heard of soon being stretched so thinly, where's the other ear piece?"

"It's over on the side there."

"If you need me, I'll be on the beach."

So he lays on the bed, clips the earpiece in and closes his eyes.

Instead of going to the beach, Jack goes to the library. It is his first visit. He marvels at the grandeur of the place and of course the dinosaurs in the garden through the windows at the back. There he finds Sue deeply involved in a book, "This place is amazing, you didn't say about the garden."

Sue unwillingly looks up from her book "I don't come here for company."

"They must have every book ever written here."

"I think you underestimate how many books have been written."

"Well there are more books than I have ever seen."

Sue gets back to reading her book, while Jack watches the wildlife out of the window, before climbing up one of the ladders to get a better view of the ceiling. When at the top he looks down and considers what happens if he falls in this simulation of reality. When things are so real you do not wish to try, just in case, and fear is automatic if your mind is presented with enough evidence. With infinite books and infinite choice, Jack goes to the beach instead.

The waves gently lap at the sand, and a light breeze flirts with the canopy's frills. The sun is high, casting shadow under the feet. But Jack desires a different mood. Next to the ice-cream stand a control desk sits, Jack looks it over, finding the option he wants. He moves a slider on the screen and millions of virtual miles away, the virtual sun follows his finger's movement, it arcs across the sky as Jack throws the sun into the sea. The gulls have gone and the stars twinkle. In the darkness the night lights appear.

Pink neons light the way through an alley. Half way along the narrow cobbled nook, a small bar looks a soothing retreat. Jack steps through the door into the snug and takes a look around. A well worn carpet on the floor, mediterranean plastered walls, a juke box to the left and opposite the bar, an old upright piano stands waiting for fingers. Jack has always fancied learning the piano and takes to wondering how flattering this game might be. He takes a seat on the stool and opens the lid, laces fingers and stretches his hands as a true pianist. He then proceeds to think musical thoughts as he dances his fingers across the keys. Sadly, this game has no sympathy for the tone deaf, a horrible clashing of chords and mistuned tumbling notes. The barman suggests he use the jukebox instead and puts a couple of his own coins on the bar as encouragement. Jack goes over and leans on the grubby old Jukebox, wiping the dust away, he looks through the track listings. "Who filled this juke box with such pop guff?" he mumbles to himself "You have a piano, but no blues, no jazz on the jukebox?" He picks some lesser than awful tracks, then orders a beer.

In the Library, Sue has lost interest in her book, she leaves it on the table and goes to the information desk "Could you tell me which beach Jack is on?"

The librarian tears himself away from his book to say "I will send it to the door." Then flicks through a screen and presses a button. Down the stairs, Sue opens the library door and looks at the darkness outside, then turns to see the daylight shining through the library windows, she shrugs and steps outside into the night.

Jack sits and hugs his pint of beer. He looks at the wear on the table, it appears to have had years of use, worn polish and gouge marks, he thinks of sitting on an imaginary chair in a virtual bar while he lays on a bed, in an alien cruise ship tearing through space at an unimaginable rate.

As the last of his selected songs fade from the jukebox, the bar's door opens. Jack looks up and recognises the face right away.

Jax smiles back at him. He is wearing a Hawaiian shirt and shorts, looking right at home in the Mediterranean bar setting, apart from the obvious. "Hello Jack, how are you? I thought I would see how you are, while you are still in range."

"I am fine, I thought you were Sue."

"Oh no, I am not Sue … There is something I must discuss, some tip to share."

Jax goes to the bar and orders two beers, returning to take a seat. He looks around the room, scanning, as someone with a secret, before saying "When you finish your journey, stick close to Jeak, I believe he can help you."

Jack instinctively looks around, distressed at this sudden news, then leans in closer in to Jax, "You think we are in danger?"

"Oh no, no danger, when Woodel wishes to stick to his rules and regulation, Jeak can tell you a twist, that is really all I can pass."

"Why did you tell me this now? Couldn't you leave my journey home worry free?"

"No worry at all, just stick near to Jeak at the final time aboard."

"But worry is the unknown, you opened doubt, then left it there."

"Please do not worry, if you do as I say, you will both be fine, if not, you will still be fine."

Jack looks a little flustered and shuffles in his seat before draining his glass. Just as Sue walks through the door.

Jack jumps up knocking his chair over "Hi Sue, Jax here was just catching up with our adventures, making sure we were settled in ok."

Sue gives Jack and Jax a suspicious stare and takes a seat, "What would you like Sue?" said Jax,

"Margarita seems about right."

Jax goes up and orders as Sue interrogates Jack without one word. Jack fidgets under the pressure.

Jax returns to the table "There Sue, Margarita with gritty edge for you."

"Thank you," said Sue with a hint of what the hell?

Jax hands Jack another beer and asks "How are you getting on with Woodel?"

"Not bad, he is.. different, but he did save me from being very sick. Maybe just to keep the loo tidy."

Jax laughs "Yes, he is very efficient."

Sue places her glass down and says "So, Jax, what were you telling Jack earlier?"

Jax takes a long swig of his beer, places it down and says

"Well, it has been lovely to catch up with you, but you are now going out of range. Have a lovely life, and who knows, we may meet again." And with that, instead of walking out of the bar, he reaches for his ear, flickers then disappears, leaving the question hanging in the air. "It was really nothing, a mistake, a misunderstanding, too odd to recall it. Really."

"It will come out in time."

"Yes, it'll all come out in the wash."

28

Sue and Jack leave the bar and head further into the tiny town, along the cobbled street, between overhanging buildings almost touching over their heads, into a small square, a fountain takes pride of place, where an acrobatic fish spits eternally into a shell.

The square is lit by oil lamps hanging from ornate curly posts. There are a few people in the square talking and laughing, couples mostly. Jack says to Sue "I wonder if any of these people are real?"

"They are all human, so probably not," Sue replies, then takes a seat on a bench and admires the clocks in a shop. Jack notes "See all the clocks read exactly the same time? Maybe the simulation is too perfect."

"Looks like it is getting late," said Sue,

"Yes I'm getting hungry, maybe a restaurant is open."

"Think we had better get some real food, it must be lunch time."

Jack laughs and says, "Oh yes, my mind got a bit absorbed there."

As they switch off their earpieces, they fade from the square and sit up in bed a moment, to let their heads return to reality.

In the dining hall, Jeak has opened the window shutter, so while they eat, they can watch infinity pour past the window. Jeak asks "Did you enjoy your time in the machine?"

Jack checks with Sue momentarily, then says "Yes, it was nice, an interesting evening. For a morning."

"I am glad you enjoyed it," said Jeak.

Woodel Interrupts "This afternoon, you may use the exercise equipment."

He had sneaked in from nowhere behind Sue and Jack. Jack jerks his head around with a crack, "Ouch, I mean, yes, thank you, that would be interesting." Woodel introduces an awkward quiet to the dining room. They finish their lunch and let it settle in stony silence.

In the exercise room Jack is honouring his promise to give it a go, and Sue is there for the entertainment. As in any gymnasium there are machines in a bare room. Woodel would have this place no other way than spotless. There is still a hint of body odour in the air. Woodel goes to a panel on the wall and presses some buttons, making the walls burst into life. Now the machines are no longer in a room, they are in a forest clearing. Candy floss clouds float overhead and deer like animals browse leaves on the bushes.

The sound of birds singing fill the ears, yet the faint gym smell remains. Sue takes an exaggerated sniff with a sour face. Woodel notes this and states "The ozone presenter is not yet repaired." Jack eyes the nearest machine, four arms protrude with padded cups and a saddle resides in the centre. Woodel guides Jack into the exercise machine and the cups grip his feet and his hands and the machine proceeds to start to push and pull his limbs in wild bends and extensions. While Jack tries to remain in the saddle, he grunts and he groans, as he is treated as a child treats a Stretch Armstrong. "Ok, thats enough," says Sue, "turn it off."

"It is usual to exercise for longer.."

"Off!" Sue demands.

Woodel turns the machine off and Jack slumps into the saddle as the machine releases his limbs. Sue helps Jack from the machine, wrapping an arm around his shoulder, walking him through the surreal door alone in the forest. Sue ignores Woodel asking if she would like to try it out.

Jeak meets them in the hall and Sue remarks "Your friend, he's a lunatic." Jeak looks aghast and goes to find out what Woodel has done. Woodel is writing on his note pad, "What did you do to Jack, he can hardly walk?" (Jeak asked this in his own tongue of course, and it sounded much harsher in Ilena). "They were outside of health limits, I believed they needed exercise. Only the usual exercise."

"But humans don't exercise like that, they do not work that way."

In the Ilena's way, the body is pushed to beyond it's limit in every way, before they go to the doctor and heal the damage, each time they exercise the body gets much stronger and more flexible, as it is tortured and repaired.

Jack is slumped across a table in the restaurant, as Sue tries to work the water machine. "Let me," says Jeak, and pours a glass, "Come, I shall get Jack better in the medical room, I am sorry for my co-part's misjudgement."

Jack is returned to the medical bay once again and he lays down on the bed. Jeak passes the fan beam over him, this time more slowly, to assess his joints. Sue comforts Jack, stroking his forehead. She says to Jeak "He had better not have broken him." Jeak's look of concern fades as he looks at the dials flicker into happier zones, "Do not worry, he is going to be better than ever, and even able to touch his toes!"

Over dinner Jack is beaming, his back straighter than ever and his hip soreness is gone, though Sue quashes his suggestion of having another go. "That machine is a death-trap, any longer and you would have been torn apart!"

Jeak approaches the table and takes a seat, he picks at Jack's leftovers as he says "It is good to see you looking so well, we are likely to be arriving back to your planet tomorrow, after a short stop for fuel."

Sue eyes the greedy fingers and says "Quite an economical ship then. You hungry?"

Jeak hold his hands up "Oh, no thank you, I am full." Then says "Do you have any last requests?" He eyes the faces of Jack and Sue then adds "Of things to do before you leave us, it is only a short time." Jack lets out a small sigh, then scratches his chin and looks to Sue "Can we take any mementos with us? Such as a bottle of drink?"

Jeak glances to the sides, for any possible listening ears, then he replies "Woodel would know, then all would know, it would be a universal incident, so maybe not." He brightens and says "But you can drink as much as you wish while you are here."

The three of them retire to the bar, Jeak is getting some tumblers and fiddling with switches, before he finds the one he wants. The ship's crisp clean white lines disappear in a snap and behind the bar is the ocean, the waves teasing the sand of the beach on a calm evening, the bar is now a rustic tiki bar, with a roof of straw. The chairs now bamboo, though when they walk the sand moves but is not felt, the ground still feels metal, the bar's edges are not where they seem, though the ozone presenter is working here, so the sea's aroma wafts through the nostrils. Jeak says "It is not quite the same as the VR machine, but not bad, to give a little mood, and we get to drink real drinks."

They sit and sip and soak up the relaxed mood, they ignore the door opening in the middle of nowhere, and ignore Woodel making notes, then ignore him leaving.

A wandering musician arrives and just as he is starting to play, Jeak turns him off. They settle quietly and get a little tipsy again while listening to the shush of the shore.

29

Three empty bottles sit on the table and a sense of relaxation permeates the bar, Jack has a sudden realisation, and decides to show off to his mate "Look what I can do Sue!" he says and sits himself down into the splits with his new limber legs. "That's useful Jack, can you get up?"

"Oh yes," he says then flops to the side and pulls his legs together, "See!." Jack declares his love for Sue several times, and his love for Jeak twice. Jeak is always ready for a drink and fun, but somehow he manages to still do everything he needs to do too. Such as directing Jack away from trying to pee behind a nonexistent bush and showing where the door to the toilet is. This also includes getting his guests to their bed, to sleep off their last intergalactic celebration.

The next morning the ship's lights seem brighter than ever, as the three sit eating a second bowl of hangover porridge. The window screen is open and the infinite twinkle is flowing past a little slower, as they are slowing to refuel.

The ship stops and Woodel goes about the business of refuelling elsewhere out of sight. The lights dim, then darken entirely. To allow Jack and Sue to stand and admire the stars in this part of the universe. The clarity is again astounding, no twinkle created by the atmosphere's wobble, no blur, no distortion. Just crystal clear lights from infinite suns. Each hosting planets and each planet with their moons. In hours they would return to their planet, orbiting around one pinprick in an endless glittery blanket.

Momentarily the ships begins to accelerate, in no time at all the stars start to glide, Jack says "Imagine how fast we must be traveling that stars so far away start to move past the window." Behind, Jeak points out, "If you turn around, they are instantly all at your back." The lights come back up and the window blind closes. Jeak clears the table, as Sue pops to the loo. Normality in the extraordinary.

These are the final moments of a journey, where the mind is in limbo, no longer settled into the trip, as the mind is already at the destination and planning. Jack and Sue are in the lounge flicking through dinner menus when Jeak comes in. "We are making our approach to your planet, would you like to see?"

Jack pops up, "Already? Of course!" Sue orders on the menu, just in case, then gets up to join them. They walk through the corridor to a lift they have not used before, emerging onto the flight deck. It is a huge room compared to that of the saucer, with an expansive sweeping window. The controls are vast and multi coloured, with just two seats, looking as lonely as children's chairs in a ballroom.

Jeak takes a seat, his hands a blur across the controls, but little seems to be happening. Woodel arrives and takes a seat in the other chair, placing his pad down. Sue looks amazed, as she had presumed it was attached. Woodel joins in with the digit dance across the control panel. Still they seem to just be elegantly gliding forwards.

When in the centre of the window a recognisable tiny blue marble appears. Slowly it swells, so slowly it is barely perceptible as the ship continues to decelerate.

Transfixed they watch home draw nearer. How innocent she looks from here, peacefully playing with the moon.

Nerves start to jangle as the earth now fills the screen, the clouds tumble over continents and oceans twinkle in the sun. Now Jeak holds the control sticks and they begin the descent. Briefly, a dancing orange flame washes across the screen, soon replaced with Earth gravity's vibrations. Familiar blue skies and wisps of cloud flicking past. They play among the clouds, then they chase the morning back into the dark, back where night still looms.

The cities are never asleep, their twinkle tries to ape the stars above. Between two cities then between two towns, silently the ship finds a nook to land in nowhere.

A collective breath is taken, before Jeak pops out of his chair. "We must get things done quickly, come along." And he hurries out of the flight deck, beckoning Sue and Jack to hurry along. By the time they hurry to the hanger, they are both out of breath from all the hurrying. Recovering breath they watch Jeak press some controls on a console. A portion of the floor begins to slide away, revealing a glimpse of home land below. Jeak turns to Jack and says "Sorry, you'll have to pilot it out." So Jack gets in old faithful Betsy, the keys are still hanging from the ignition, a strange foreign familiarity sweeps through him, before he gets his head together and tries to start her. Against all his thoughts of embarrassment, she starts first time. In fact better than she ever has, he edges her forwards and looks with trepidation down the steep loading ramp, the throttle now a lever for power this car had never known before, tyres screech on the slick floor, till Jack backs off and feathers the throttle, holding the car back with the brake, gently guiding her back to earth. Jack gets out and looks up the ramp to wave Sue down, but she is nowhere to be seen. So Jack clambers up the ramp to find her, and of course, it is good manners to say goodbye.

When he has managed to scrabble to the top, he sees Sue is at the back of the hanger and Woodel has arrived, a memory suddenly pops into Jacks head, 'Jeak! I've got to stick to Jeak'. So he sticks to him and waves for Sue to come over, "Come over Sue, to say our goodbyes." Sue looks a little perturbed. Jack tells "There seems to be some sort of formality before we leave." Woodel leaves the three alone, as he fetches something. When sure he is away, Jeak explains, "You must be cleansed with this machine before you may leave. Think of oranges while it is in use. Don't ask me how I know, just think of oranges. Oranges." They both look confused at this turn of events. Sue says "We were saying goodbye, and now oranges?.."

"Shhhhh!" says Jeak as Woodel returns with two sticks with boxes on the end.

Jack whispers to Sue "Oranges oranges." Just as Woodel holds the sticks up to them and they both go stiff as boards. Eyes glaze and hearts judder. Jeak never likes this bit.

Woodel twists crystal controls on the sticks and gaseous lights emit from the boxes. The lights fade and Woodel writes a note.

Jeak approaches Jack and puts a hand on his shoulder, "Right, time to get you back in your Vehicle." Jeak holds Jack under the shoulder and pulls him back, "Take his legs," he squeaks. Carefully they shuffle down the ramp as

Jack swings to and fro between them, in some odd plastic slumber. They sit him in the car and climb the ramp to retrieve Sue.

Now both in the car, Jeak leans in and says "Sorry about this, goodbye, great to meet you, I hope you are thinking of oranges." With that he closes the door and climbs back up the ramp. Even for a race as advanced and healthy as the Ilena, he has had enough of going up and down this ramp.

In a few moments the ramp begins to close, in a few moments more, the ship silently gathers to take its own weight and floats into the air like the ground letting go of a balloon. There is the slightest disturbance in the air as the ship shrinks to a dot, then is gone.

30

Sue and Jack sit, stone still staring into the distance. Jack is sat on the seatbelt stalk, he will be uncomfortable soon, but for now only oranges fill his mind. First Sue begins to rouse from the stupor, but remains still, in shock, as Jack snorts awake and wonders what is digging in his behind.

They look out into the field, into the darkness, then around them. In the mirror Jack sees in the gloom, an unbroken fence. Things do not add up, large parts of there to here are missing. They look at each other, Jack says "It looks like we survived, lets get to John's house." Sue gathers a little thought and says "Yes, we are already very late."

They bump along by the edge of the rutted field, trying to find a gap, after ten minutes they find a gate and get back on the road. Sue recognises a church, they regain their bearings and in a fit of ferocity Betsy launches down the road, scaring the pair of them. "Wow she is really enjoying the cool air," says Jack.

"Take it easy," says Sue.

As they get to residential areas they start to notice how brightly lit the houses are. Red and orange lights hang in trees and some have brightly lit Santa Clauses in their garden. Sue shakes her head "It gets earlier every year, it's getting ridiculous, can we at least let summer go first?"

As they pull into John's driveway they see some lights along the guttering here too, but the house lights are off. "We are so late, they have gone to bed." said Sue.

Jack still confused says "Should we just leave them to sleep or apologise first?"

"Oh we are going in, it has been a long journey."

They ring the bell. Then they ring it again. Eventually some lights come on in a back room and John appears at the door. He looks tired, shocked and dazed "Mum? Dad? where have you been?!" Sue is a little taken aback at the over reaction "We had a small incident on the way, sorry we are late."

John stutters "B.. b.. but it's nearly Christmas.."

Over the night it sinks in slowly that a large part of their year has gone missing into the ether. Which understandably leaves all rather shocked. Later over a stiff drink Jack asks "How are Jenny and Sean? They must have missed your mother." John looks down and sighs, he hugs his father, "Sorry, but Sean is no longer here, he, he took his own life. It was the drugs, the company. I'm sure it would not have been different had you been here." Jack slumps into the couch. Sue sits by his side and hides into the crook of his neck, both disorientated and distressed.

John tries to console them, "Jenny is marrying Pamela, so that is lovely, and Julie is expecting."

But so much has hit them in the face, more just washes past them at this moment.

Over the next two weeks, there are talks with the police, and a remembrance service for Sean.

Now it is Christmas eve.

The decorations are all glowing brightly, the presents are ripe to bursting under the tree, outside in the cool evening, no snow is falling to bless this Christmas, but the breath billowing out of cold faces reminds all of the time of year. The family sit around the table. Beers reside, alongside snacks and the odd bowl of fruit for the ones still looking after themselves, even at Christmas. There is reason to celebrate, but Sue and Jack are feeling somewhat empty still. Sue takes an orange and passes one to Jack. They sit and look at their laps as they dig their nails into the peel, Sue always good at this, removing the peal in one long strand, as Jack picks away in untidy lumps. Through neatness and oafishness they reach the same destination and take a segment out of the orange and chew. Looking down at the peel and tasting the fruit. Visions of ships and planets pour back into place. They glance at each other for reassurance that they are both feeling it, both having the same rebirth into wonderful memories.